Moss,
Mallards
and Mules

Moss, Mallards and Mules

and Other Hunting and Fishing Stories

Bob Brister

Illustrated by Stanley Farnham

WINCHESTER PRESS

Text copyright © 1969 by Jim V. McConkey
Illustrations copyright © 1973 by Bob Brister
All rights reserved

Library of Congress Catalog Card Number: 73–78819
ISBN 0–87691–113–0

Published by Winchester Press
460 Park Avenue, New York 10022

Printed in the United States of America

Contents

Preface

Few things are rarer than quality outdoor fiction. One can think of a handful of fine writers—Hemingway and Ruark spring to mind—who also truly knew the outdoors and could convey its essence in print. From the other side, there have been a select few outdoorsmen who also happened to be gifted storytellers, and who, happily for us, were willing to lay aside rod and gun long enough to put something of their knowledge and insight between hard covers. A Nash Buckingham or Hal Sheldon belongs in this category.

There can be no question about Bob Brister's skills as an outdoorsman. Anyone who has ever watched him shoot skeet, trap or live birds, handle a bateau, bass boat or casting rod, rig for marlin or work a flat for redfish will know that he has few peers in any of these activities. And frankly, though I have been privileged to share a blind, boat or trail with some of the top outdoorsmen of our era, I can think of nobody to match his degree of expertise across the whole spectrum of gunning and angling skills.

Of more importance to the reader, however, is the fact that Bob can also write—and one need only turn a page or two to appreciate how deftly he can weave a spell with words. Yes, *Moss, Mallards and Mules* reveals both that Brister can write and that *he has been there,* and he narrates the tales that make up this fine collection with such accuracy and feeling that he virtually takes the reader along with him, step by step, cast by cast, and shot by shot.

I have a suspicion that I will return to this marvelous book time and again over the coming years.

Grits Gresham
Natchitoches, Louisiana
July 1973

Moss, Mallards and Mules

The acorns had begun to fall around Uncle William's shack at
the edge of the Trinity River bottoms, and cold rain had moist-
ened the red and brown leaves and left the air fresh and crisp in
the early mornings.

Uncle William was behind the barn, hitching up the wood
wagon, and I was waiting to go with him because not even the
old Ford pickup with the mud-grip tires could get down into that
black-gumbo bottom after a rain.

In those days Uncle William and I had a sort of unwritten

agreement; certain staples such as Blue Ribbon Malt Extract, empty gallon jugs, and occasionally a length of copper tubing were quietly brought to him from town.

In exchange, he took along and tolerated a somewhat precocious white boy in the throes of learning about hunting, fishing, girls and hound dogs. And he did so with the total discipline of age and authority.

"You jess as well leave thet shotgun to the house," he warned. "Today is wood-cuttin' an' line-settin' day, an' you know duck season don't open til Sattidy."

A finger-in-nose delegation of jet-black small fry poured out of the shack to look me over, stairstepped proof of prolificacy for an old man in his seventies who had children as young as some of his grandchildren.

Two or three of them were jumping up and down, pointing toward the barn and what was obviously a developing conflict between Uncle William and a mule named Rodney.

"Lookit ole Roahd-nay go," they chanted in glee. "He sho gonna git hainted now!"

Rodney's mind was apparently made. He reared, backed up, kicked the barn . . . stirring out a cackling procession of setting hens, pigeons, and squealing hogs . . . and with his ears laid back defied Uncle William to force the bit into his mouth.

"Haint him!" the rooting section chanted. "Haint him now, wheah we kin watch!"

I had heard the word "haint" used by colored folk referring to ghosts or spirits. After all, the logical thing to haunt something would be a "haint." But I didn't grasp this usage.

"You ain't never seen Uncle William haint nothin'?" one of the older boys whooped gleefully. "He kin put haints in anythin', bad haints. Las' summer he hainted a lizard fo' us, an' dat lizard clumb straight up de chimney an' jumped off lak' a flyin' squrrul!"

About that time Uncle William began making some strange sounds, in a tongue unknown to me, and suddenly he jumped back and raised both hands high over his head.

Rodney stood there a minute. He sneezed mightily. He lay

down in the corral mud and rolled over twice, kicking all four legs straight up into the air as if trying to run upside down, braying and bawling at the top of his lungs. Then he rolled over, shook himself, and stood placidly while Uncle William harnessed him to the wagon.

We climbed in and rattled off toward the timber, no questions asked, because Uncle William would discuss haints only if he wanted to anyway, and Rodney had become a paragon of pulling power.

In the foreboding darkness of the moss-draped cypress, mists were rising from the brown current of the river. Giant alligator gars rolled, and the overhanging willows, vines and semitropical vegetation might as well have been the Amazon. I would not have gone in that bottom on a dark day without Uncle William.

He cut through the woods, dodging the low places, and finally stopped the wagon a long way off as he always did when he was coming to his "cookin' place." I had to sit in the wagon and wait; he didn't want any witnesses nor wagon tracks to his "kitchen."

He came back presently, rolling a big oaken barrel. He never dumped the mash near the still for several reasons, one being that he always had something else to do with it.

"I ought to put dis heah in de perch hole wheah we cut dem new willows," he said. "Perch likes it moah'n people. But you's got youself in such a fizz to go duck huntin' we maybe better take it over to de slough."

"Will ducks eat that stuff?"

"Will dey eat it? Boy, once dey gets a taste of it, dey all but starves lookin' fo' mo'. Dem mallets gits high as a minister in a hoah house on a little of dis 'stuff,' as you calls it."

Without looking at him, I knew Uncle William had finally decided I was old enough for man talk, because it was the first time he had ever mentioned a minister in a whorehouse, and also the way he said it meant he was ready to answer some of the questions I had been asking for a long time.

"How old is yoah runnin' buddy, Richard, now?"

"Fifteen, I think."

"An' you keep botherin' me wantin' to know what wrong wid him an' how come he won't go coon huntin' wid us no mo'. You don't notice him hangin' 'round dat li'l Smith girl?"

"What's that got to do with coon hunting?"

"Enough dat he ain't got time fo' no coons rat now. Ain't nothin' wrong wid ole Dick; he jess cockstruck."

"How can you keep that from happening to you?"

"Well, you kin not ever git to be mo' than foteen, or you could try an' jump a bobwire fence an' not quite make it, or you could git youself some li'l ole girl just because she a girl an' not git sweet on her. But since you ain't gonna do none o' dem things, best way is to stay outa town till you know what to do 'bout dat problem."

"I know already."

"Uh huh; you thinks you knows. No man knows nothin' 'bout thet till he git thirty-five, an' after thet he just find out how little he do know."

"Well then, why do I have to learn it all the hard way, why can't you just tell me what is the best kind of girl to have and all that? You've had enough of 'em."

He grunted, belly bobbing in the overalls, and spit a stream of snuff. "You jess looks fo' de one dat make you think you really doin' somethin' to her; if dat be good enough, she likely git to be-lievin' it, too."

He reached beneath the wagon seat, pulled out the clear, half-gallon jug with the handle on it, and threw up his left arm to cradle the jug, pulling three deliberate, sucking swallows around the dip of snuff.

Then he screwed the lid back on, ignoring the request I had already made a hundred times.

"You gits a sip o' dat when you gits old enough to handle it an' know what to do wid it. The very devil in dat jug, boy, an' he git out if you ain't ready fo' him."

The mules bogged down to their bellies a couple of times crossing the river end of the duck slough, and half a dozen mallards exploded out of the button willows well within shotgun range. I wished mightily for the .410.

He got out of the wagon, picked up the crosscut saw, and motioned for me to take the other end. As we worked, I couldn't help but ask why he had to pick a great big pecan of a squirrel tree, right at the end of the slough, when there were hundreds of trees right by the edge of the bottom, not doing anybody any good.

"Fo' one thing, pecan wood happen to be de best fo' several purposes, one bein' to smoke sausages, an' fo' another thing, dis heah tree dead anyway, if you didn't notice, 'cause the moss choke it to death, an' fo' another thing we is rat now makin' a li'l white boy a cinch place to kill hisself a mallet duck next Sattidy, lessen he don't keep on pesterin' de brains o' dis outfit.

"You notice a quail or duck in de bresh; very fust thing he think 'bout before he jump is how he gonna git outta der widout gettin' tangled up in de limbs. He pick out de best openin' an' go right out it every time. We jess made ourselves de best openin' on dis slough, an' every duck on it gonna come out clost 'nough wheah even a white boy wid a .410 can worry one to death as dey goes by. Now come help me roll dis bar'l o' mash."

The next Saturday was a drizzling, dreary day, fitting for revelations of haints or mallards, and when we stopped the wagon in the wet underbrush Uncle William sent two of his older boys around the slough.

"Go all de way aroun' now, long way out in de bottom from de slough, an' come back up thisaway slow an' quiet. Jess play lak you all got guns staid o' sticks. Dem mallets need a chance to swim up thisaway before dey jumps."

Uncle William sauntered his girth down through the bushes without getting wet, nor making a sound, and stopped beside the big downed pecan. He backed up against a tree, dropped two shells into his old 12-gauge hammer gun with the copper wire wrapped around the stock, and told me to keep still.

Our drivers weren't making a sound. Thirty minutes passed, and a woodpecker worked diligently on the downed trunk of the dead pecan. Then suddenly a wood duck squealed, there was a muffled roar of wings, and a beautiful pair of mallard drakes were heading straight for us, wings beating, heavy necks straining to clear the trees.

Uncle William got them both, and with his shots the air was full of ducks. A beautiful wood duck drake passed, not fifteen feet from the end of the gun, but I wanted more than all else a mallard, a big greenhead.

Three hens passed and I heard Uncle William's double speak twice more and then there was the greenhead coming straight to me through the hole and I pulled the little .410 barrel out in front of him, jerked the trigger, and he dropped like a rock.

Some of the ducks were still circling, and one mallard hen was hanging right over the trees, even after all that gunfire, quacking her heart out. I started up with the gun, and Uncle William grabbed the barrel.

"She's jess a l'il tite on dat mash," he chuckled. "Someday you be tite an' maybe somebody won't kill you fo' talkin' too much."

His boys came running up excitedly, wading out in the cold water to pick up the ducks, and I stroked the green head of the biggest drake and announced that he was mine.

"No suh," Uncle William said firmly, "thass yo duck." He pointed to a scraggly little bird of a species I had never seen, with a high green topknot on his head, a narrow beak for a bill, and less than half the size of the fat mallards. But I knew I had shot a mallard; he had looked as big as a goose up there, white breast shining against the dark cypress trees.

I turned over the little duck, and his breast was white, and under his wings was white. But he was not a mallard.

The little boys gathered around. "Did you haint dat duck, pappa? Look how he done drawed up to wheah his head don't fit his feathers no mo'; pappa done shrunk dat duck!"

Uncle William's belly was bouncing inside the overalls, but he didn't say anything until we were halfway home, and the boys had picked the ducks as we went, talking among themselves but afraid to pick the "hainted" one.

"Ain't much to haintin' things fo' dem younguns," he said, speaking low and watching to see, the boys didn't hear.

He produced the brown bottle of Garrett's Snuff from his overalls.

"Jess put a l'il pinch o' dis in a lizard's mouf, an' he plumb go wild. An' a dog dat barks at night, pshaw, one dip an' de devil got his tongue. But ole Rodney, now dat mule he takes half a handful to do right. Some powerful haints in dis one l'il jar," he grinned, "but don't you go tellin' dem younguns. Dat duck you kilt is a l'il ole trash duck, dey calls 'um mergansers o' somethin', an' dey ain't fit to eat noway; tastes lak spoilt fish."

I pondered this hainting business.

"If one of your boys wouldn't mind you sometime, you wouldn't haint him, would you?"

Uncle William looked at me sidewise. "Man carryin' a big pistol," he philosophized, "most likely never have to use it . . ."

"Naw, boy, I ain't givin' no stuff to no chillun . . . all I kin do to keep in it fo' me an' ole Rodney. Dat old mule," he chuckled, slapping the wide, bluish back lightly with the reins. "He sumptin. Dat mule ain't really been mean nor bad in three o' fo' years. He too old now. But he jess have dat tough act he go through every now an' den when he need a dip o' snuff."

A Matter of Rationale

He hadn't seen the old man in years, and it was a relief to know Mr. Dare hadn't changed much, for better or for worse. They were grinding through the black Trinity river-bottom mud on the way to a couple of sloughs where Mr. Dare had taught him to bass-fish in grammar school days, and the oldtimer was in fine fettle.

"Little Dick Davidson," he grunted to himself, herding the Jeep into a harrowing succession of skids through a boghole.

"Went off to college, then to war, come home and got married, and finally he's ready to go fishin' again. Shame a man has to waste all that fishin' time."

"Didn't waste it all," Dick grinned. "Learned enough, in fact, to beat the old master, probably, if he's as hardheaded as he used to be and won't use the plastic worm."

Mr. Dare spat contemptuously, as if the slimy word triggered tobacco juice.

"That's a shame," he said finally, "for a while there it looked like you might amount to somethin'."

"So what's wrong with fishing the worm?"

"Nothin', except maybe what it does to a man's character."

He swerved out of some deep ruts, darting the rattling, rusted apparition around a clump of palmetto bushes.

"Fished with a worm man one time; never'll do it again if I know about it in time," he mused, glancing at Dick meaningfully. "It was years ago, up in Arkansas on the Buffalo, where a creek came into the river, and he had brought along his little blind brother.

"The creek was muddy, so we put the blind boy on the bank where the muddy water was mixin' with the clear river, and caught him a couple of little green frogs so he could bottom-fish. Before we even got back to the boat, the kid had caught a three-pound smallmouth and missed another one. So we stopped to watch, and the kid put on his last frog, which was considerable bigger than the others, and cast back out again, probably havin' the most fun he'd ever had in his life. But that big frog just came swimmin' back to the top and got out and climbed up on a log and sat there."

"So what does that prove about worm fishermen?"

"I'm comin' to that," Mr. Dare glared triumphantly. "For a solid hour that feller bumped his damn worm all over that hole the kid had been fishing, caught three good bass, and all the time lettin' his poor blind brother sit there with his bait out of the water thinkin' he was fishin'. Now that," he spat again, "is a worm fisherman for you."

"It isn't my fault you happened to fish with one guy like that who used the worm," Dick argued, "and it isn't my fault that bass will hit those baits when they won't take anything else. I didn't invent the worm."

"It's not your fault about dynamite either, is it, boy?" the old man chuckled. "But I guess you'd use it if that's what it took to beat me."

He stopped the Jeep at the tail end of the button willows marking the upper slough, and Dick threw the canvas-covered tube over his shoulder and cut straight through the woods.

The Trinity bottoms hadn't changed much, either, the gaunt moss-draped elms along the bluff banks of the river, with greening oaks and pecans marking the low country leading to the

slough, and clumps of razor-sharp palmettos to keep a man's feet carefully on the trail. Finally he found the thick button willows marking the slough, and saw there were no fresh human signs in the rich, black mud, only the tracks of coon, deer and the wild feral pigs which have roamed these bottoms for generations.

The slough had once been an oxbow curve of the Trinity, long since cut off from the main stream, stocked by spring floods when the muddy river backed into it, full of gars, gators, cottonmouth moccasins, and linesided black bass whose ancestors had never seen a hatchery.

The old man had his theories about them too. "These are wild bass, son," he'd said, "a gentleman's fish. Not them damn hatchery-fed idiots like in them new lakes."

Dick dropped the tube into the shallow water, carefully stepped into the leg holes, and sat down, feeling the cool water rise up above the waist of his waders, and a flood of memories returned with the musky smell of riverbottom mud and the dank, swampish water.

There was a dark shadowed lane between two willows, and he kicked silently toward it, tying on a black plastic worm, rigged weedlessly so that the hook point was buried in the plastic.

He turned the tube into position, cast far back into the lane, and saw the worm hang for a second on an outcropping limb. Then it dropped into the water, and the surface swirled. He kicked backward, lowering the rod to take up slack, then struck back so hard the tube tipped dangerously.

The bass lunged for the brush, but the heavy twenty-pound monofilament turned him. The water churned and boiled, and after two wild jumps a long, green-striped patriarch of the slough turned belly up and was lifted from the water, tail curled in exhaustion. Dick felt a twinge of conscience about the heavy line, but that's what it takes to drive a hook point through a plastic worm and into a fish. All the pros used it that way.

On the other slough, the old man was fishing as he had always fished, the light-tipped bamboo rod effortlessly flicking the small white plug within inches of the shoreline, tiny, braided eight-pound tournament line whirring softly off the reel and starting back as the plug descended, allowing it to touch the water as lightly as a falling leaf.

He had whittled the plug himself, the same model for thirty-five years, painted with pearl fingernail polish, the eyes a carefully tinted and blended baby blue. For some reason bass liked that combination, or maybe he did. He'd been kidded about it for years, his old "Baby Blue Eyes," but the kidding rarely lasted long when the stringers were compared at the end of the day.

The little plug sat cockily at rest, ripples departing from it, and he made it dip slightly, kicking and twitching seductively toward a gnarled black stump with dark fingers of roots clutching down into the water. A thick black moccasin writhed out of the roots and swam out to the plug, looked at it curiously, then saw the old man and dived underwater.

It was on the sixth cast that the plug hit one of the roots, was masterfully flipped clear, and the instant it met the water the surface exploded and the light rod bent dangerously.

"All right now," the old man said out loud, spitting a powerful stream in concentration, "let's see what you can do."

Unfettered by the light pressure of rod and line, the bass came out high and clear on the first jump, gills flaring, hooks on the plug rattling in midair, and the old man leaned back into the tube to take out just enough slack to keep him from throwing the lure.

The bass surged for the protection of the limbs, the rod bent more dangerously, and he came up again, slashing and blasting the surface.

The old man was savoring every moment of it, every surge of the rod, sensing what the fish would do and countering before he could do it. Finally the bass was whipped, belly up and gasping, and the old man respectfully picked him up by the lower lip.

"Just couldn't take that tormentin' topwater no longer, could you, old feller?" he said to the fish, carefully checking the hooks on Baby Blue Eyes. "I hope you'd have had sense enough not to hit a damn worm; who ever heard of an old gentleman bass foolin' with a worm?"

He kicked down the shoreline, and found three more good

bass, obviously on nests, which would only swirl the plug, not take it. And it troubled him. They were likely females, not yet spawned, and they would be big. They also, he pondered, might have taken a worm. He figured bass hit that infernal plastic contraption because it looked like a snake, not a worm.

Spawning she-bass are hell on snakes and he figured they hit 'em just to get 'em away from the nest.

He spat the plug of tobacco into the water, watched it settle into the murky depths, took out his false teeth and washed them in the water, slurping a mouthful of it around inside to clean out the bits and pieces, and then studied the situation.

In decision, a little sadly, he began kicking back to the dark hole under some willows where the first bass had swirled the plug and refused it. "Sorry, young man," he grinned to himself, thinking of how cocky a boy gets out of college. "But you ain't had a lesson in some years now."

He reached into a shirt pocket and produced a wooden stick wrapped with twenty-pound monofilament, gauged the distance from the willow limbs to the water, and cut a length of the line. In the other pocket he found the small metal box of bucktail bass bugs, carefully tied by the same hands as Baby Blue Eyes, big, bushy, black bugs resembling nothing in particular, but fluffy and natural to the touch.

He tied on a bug, checked the sharpness of the big hook buried in the bucktail, and stood up in the tube to tie to a limb, careful to make sure the bug hung no more and no less than an inch above the water, so that when the wind blew it would hover just over the surface, sometimes dappling and brushing the water as the wind blew the willows.

Then he kicked down the shoreline, noted the swirl of each bass as he approached their nests, and tied his monofilament to the limbs above. He had half a dozen bugs and he used them all.

Then he went on fishing the upper end of the slough, and once while Blue Eyes was lying at rest beside a big cypress stump, he distinctly heard the slurping splash of a bass hitting on the shoreline, then other splashes and crashes of a willow limb thrashing. He smiled to himself. "That's one."

Dick had worked his slough out perfectly except for a couple of mistaken strikes which hung logs on bottom instead of bass. He had six fish, three keepers, but three in the four- or five-pound class, all spawning females.

Shortly before noon, he gave up and hitched the wet tube over his shoulder and walked straight across the bottoms to the other slough.

The old man was caught by surprise; he was about to pick up the last bass lying quietly in willow-limb captivity, and when he heard the swish of waders behind him he quickly cast Baby Blue Eyes out beside a stump and began fishing carefully and slowly, turning as if in surprise when Dick spoke.

"All right, let's see 'em."

The old man kicked back to the shoreline, away from the willow with the hooked bass under it, and creakily stepped up on shore, dragging the long stringer behind him. There were seven big bass on it, one well over six pounds.

Dick stared, swallowed, and in that moment the bass under the willow decided to make one last fight for freedom, lashed the surface, and the willow limb bucked and thrashed.

"What the hell's going on over there?"

"Well, since you're a mite younger'n me," the old man suggested, "how about finishing up running my emergency lines?"

It was then that Dick saw the glint of sunlight on monofilament.

"Well, you old bastard! You of all people! Giving me all those lectures about sportsmanship, and smart bass over dumb ones, and how you wouldn't use a worm. And what you've been doing all these years is running some kind of drop lines!"

"It ain't my fault," the old man said, eyes twinkling mischievously. "I didn't plant them willow trees there."

The Trial of Job

Frank Ramsey was looking for a lost bull in the Brush Creek pasture when he saw the distant figure stumbling in the tall grass in the rain, falling and staggering up again. He slammed on the brakes, backed the Jeep for a better look, and shoved the battered gray Stetson back on his forehead in disgust.

It was that teen-aged little girl of Jim Slaughter's two miles from home in the rain, trying to carry a bird dog puppy almost as big as she was. He watched her stumble, struggling to get the dog up into her arms again.

He'd warned that Slaughter twice about using this pasture for a dog training preserve! There were three good coveys of birds along the edge of the ricefield, and every year by the time the season opened Slaughter would have 'em so spooked they'd fly half a mile when they jumped.

He pulled on his slicker and crossed through the fence to meet the girl. Least he could do would be to give the poor thing a ride home, and it would give him another chance to warn Slaughter about that pasture. Next time, he'd let the sheriff do the talking.

The girl was too worn out to be afraid, wet white T-shirt sticking to skinny, shivering ribs as starved-looking as the stave-sided puppy's.

"Gee, thanks, Mr. Ramsey," she piped. "I had to cut across your field because the pup couldn't walk no more and I just couldn't carry him the long way around to home. He's got something terrible wrong with him, Mr. Ramsey, he does all right for a while, and then his back legs just quit on him and he can't walk a step."

Ramsey threw his heavy coat over her shoulders, and ground the Jeep through the mud to the main road, wondering what had happened to the puppy and also how such a fragile little girl could ever have been sired by Jim Slaughter.

"That old colored man, Joe, over across the creek gave him to me," she chattered, chilled to the bone. "Said he just took up around their house, and Joe's hound dogs was about to starve him to death, fightin' him off the table scraps."

The puppy looked blankly out the window, weak back legs quivering.

"His name is Job," she added, "you know, like in the Bible. Mamma named him that 'cause he had so many things wrong with him, sores and mange and stuff like ole Job had to put up with."

Slaughter wasn't home when they rolled into the trash-strewn yard, with the row of dilapidated kennels in the back and half a dozen pointers and setters chained to the clothesline by their choke collars.

Ramsey couldn't stand the sight of those dogs chained up; Jim Slaughter was a pretty fair dog trainer, and he'd won some trials, but the dogs he turned out lacked the spark a big-running dog should have; they very likely had had it chained and beaten out of them.

"Tell you what, little lady," he said. "Anytime you want to use that back pasture over there to work your pup that's just fine. But you tell your daddy I don't want to see his sorry face on my property again!"

"Yessir."

Suddenly Ramsey felt ashamed of himself. She couldn't help what her father did.

"I got a couple of pups just gettin' started," he said. "I might come over and train with you sometime; my boy needs to see somebody like you handle a dog. I've heard you're a better trainer than Jim."

"Thanks," she smiled, embarrassed but excited at the thought of having that pasture with all the quail in it for Job. "I'll sure help you any way I can, Mr. Ramsey."

It was well into the fall before he saw her again, and it was difficult to believe it was the same dog or the same girl. The pup was filled out and boisterous, and the girl was beginning to blossom into womanhood. She should be wearing a bra, he decided, but it was doubtful Jim Slaughter had noticed much of anything but the waitress in the beer joint down the road, and the old lady was likely too tired and sick to care much about this one; she had three smaller ones to worry about.

The girl was working Job with a rope, letting him get started running good, running along beside him and stepping on the rope when she yelled "whoa" just enough to let him get the idea.

Ramsey put down his own two dogs, and let them run while he walked over to watch Job. He was still puppyish and a little clumsy in the hind end, but when he began getting "birdy" at the end of the fencerow, he carried a merry, high tail, and when he

came down on point he locked up with the high-curving tail and taut, trembling stance of the classic pointer.

"You watch this," she whispered. "That dog's got the dangedest nose I ever saw; now he's winded those birds three bushes down toward the end; I saw one run in there."

She clicked softly and encouraged Job on. He crept forward as if stepping on hot cinders, nose high to catch the wind. "Careful," she said, "whoa." The dog stopped in midstride, one foot up. "Okay, easy now."

Ramsey couldn't believe his eyes. He guessed the dog's age at about ten months, but he was handling like a champion. And she'd been right about the covey; even with the drought and the grass heavy and dusty, Job had winded that covey at thirty yards! When he made a slight curving sidle ahead to cut them off, and then came down frozen, it was a sight to see. The girl's face was flushed with excitement. "You walk in to bust 'em," she said. "I want to see how he handles around strangers."

Ramsey eased up past the dog, kicked the bush, and the brown bombshells exploded all around him. Job was quivering, but steady. Then a sleeper flushed almost under his nose, and he took off after it as only a puppy can. "Whoa!" she yelled, and he stopped in midstride, looking back as if to apologize.

For the next three weeks, they trained together almost every day, and Ramsey brought along his oldest son, Sammy, who promptly proved exactly what his father had suspected. Sammy was sixteen, and he couldn't take his eyes off the girl long enough to work the dogs. It embarrassed them both, but Ramsey figured a little case of puppy love wouldn't hurt either, and he wanted the boy to get a little more interested in dogs and girls than hotrods and cigarettes.

It was in early November, just before quail season, when Ramsey's worst fears were realized. The girl showed up at their house, eyes red from crying, and stood at the back door sobbing.

"He done it," she said, "he sold Job."

Ramsey had known all along that if Jim Slaughter ever saw that dog work, and needed some money, he'd sell him in a second. And Slaughter always needed money.

"Who bought him?"

"Feller named Logan is all I know. Daddy claimed he didn't sell him, that the man showed up and claimed Job was his all the time and had the papers to prove it. Said he lost him when he was a puppy."

More likely, Ramsey figured, Slaughter had tried to sell the dog, and the man had recognized him and produced his papers. He'd noticed Job had a tongue tattoo, and he was bound to have belonged to someone.

Ramsey invited her inside, and picked up the phone. He knew this man Logan well. He kept a kennel of top dogs and did a lot of business entertaining with them at his hunting lodge. Ramsey had never liked the man, and he knew money couldn't buy the dog if he'd ever seen Job work.

Logan was huffy about it at first. Sure he'd sent for the dog after his trainer identified him. Slaughter had put up a stink about it, but there was no doubt whose dog it was. He'd given Slaughter two hundred dollars to pay for the training and board, which was fair enough, wasn't it?

"Meet us over in the McLendon pasture tomorrow morning and bring your dogs," Logan boasted. "My trainer says he hasn't seen a pointer pup like this since Gunsmoke."

The morning was clear and cold, ideal for the dogs because it had rained in the night. Ramsey was waiting with Sammy and the girl when Logan's caravan arrived, the big, black Cadillac followed by a Jeep with the dog wagons.

When Logan got out, walking with the aid of a heavy, ivory-headed cane, Ramsey realized they'd be working the dogs from the Jeep, perfect for a big-running dog like Job.

The other guests, two Eastern couples, were resplendent in leather-faced hunting pants, bright-red vests, and porkpie hats decorated with field trial medals. They were talking of pedigrees and bloodlines, and Logan wasted no time bringing forth his new pride. He yelled for the handler to put down the new pup and the best of his older dogs.

When the crate opened, Job came bounding out, made a classy circle around the car, and Logan blew his whistle. But Job had seen the girl and went straight to her, whining and jumping up on her.

Logan blew his whistle again, and started walking over angrily toward the dog.

Job stopped short and looked up at the man and the crowd around him. His tail started down. His back legs began to tremble. He was looking straight at Logan, at the leather-faced pants and the big, ivory-headed cane. He sank to the ground, cowering, belly-dragging toward the girl, then turned over on his back, belly up and tail between his legs.

Logan's face was livid, his lips whitened, his hands twitched. The ladies giggled, and the men began to laugh. Ramsey laughed too, as coarsely and loudly as possible.

"Your field champion," one of the men said, "may be just a bit gunshy, old boy."

"Was gunshy," Logan muttered, carefully raising the big, knob-headed cane. At the instant before he struck, Sammy stepped forward and caught his arm and for a second they were face to face, both shaking.

Ramsey stepped between them. "If you don't want the dog," he said evenly, "I'll take him."

He took two crisp bills from his billfold. Nobody said anything. Sammy was carrying Job to Ramsey's Jeep, and the girl was behind him, racking with sobs.

When the Jeep turned onto the paved highway, the girl was crying and laughing at the same time.

"Gunshy!" she sobbed. "How many birds have you an' Sammy killed over him already? Remember the day we were shootin' all those silly pen-raised trainin' birds, all around his ears, and he never even flinched? Gunshy!"

She was sitting boylike on the seat, hugging the dog around the neck. "I reckon," she sniffed, "ole Job just never had seen all them fancy clothes before, and it plumb spooked him. He wasn't supposed to be no rich folk's dog anyway, wuz you, Job?"

"Nope," grinned Ramsey, "and right now he sure ain't. He's a partnership dog; you keep him and train him and we'll all hunt him if we can ever get Sammy to where he can hit a bird."

They laughed, Job wagged his tail and slobbered, and Ramsey told them to put him up in the big kennel behind the house. No use telling either one of them that he'd already heard what had happened to Job's back so long ago . . . nor that a puppy may get over being gunshy, but never the man, nor the ivory-headed cane, that had tried to kill him for it.

The Holy Mackerel

White wisps of fog hung low over Louisiana 23, and the head-lights of the pickup camper were beginning to play tricks upon the sleepless, reddened eyes of Jake Ratliff. Suddenly the narrow band of black asphalt was not there, the nose of the heavy truck was climbing into the air, brakes screeched, the hydraulic actua-tor brakes on six thousand pounds of boat and trailer grabbed, and the truck came down sideways with the trailer in the ditch, lean-ing but not overturned.

Mickey Finnerty bailed out of the bunk over the cab, saw Jake was okay, and jumped out the side door with the fire extinguisher and two emergency flares.

"What happened?"

Jake shook his head.

"Well, keep your fingers crossed that she'll pull that trailer out of the ditch."

Mickey climbed into the cab, gunned the big V-8 until the frame rattled, and slowly, inch by inch, as if pushed by some unseen hand, the heavy, 23-foot Deep-V boat crept forward on her trailer like a giant turtle climbing out of the ditch.

It was only when all wheels were on asphalt again, and Jake ran back to pick up the flares, that he saw the figure standing beside the road and realized someone back there had done some powerful pushing.

"Where'd you come from?" he asked thankfully. "Could we give you a ride?"

In the eerie light of the flare, the man's face was strangely serene as he smiled and made a vague motion toward the delta swamp. Jake figured he was one plenty drunk little coonass. But he got into the cab.

While Jake slept, Mickey kept talking, mostly to keep awake.

"We've trailered in from Houston to try and catch a marlin off the mouth of the river; supposed to be some great fishing out of South Pass. It's hard to realize how far this delta sticks right out into the Gulf; ten miles beyond the mouth of the river is more like fifty. We're about thirty miles offshore right now in relation to the coastline."

The stranger nodded.

"We plan to find somebody at Venice who knows the pass into the Gulf and how to get to Port Eads for bait and fuel."

"I show you the way," the stranger said softly.

Mickey did a double-take. "You know the river that well?"

"The river, and the sea."

"You ever do any deckhand work on a sportfishing boat?"

"I have been on many boats."

They were passing through Buras, beer joints blazing and Cajun music blaring at 3:00 a.m., neon glowing in the morning fog. A ship's foghorn hooted forlornly on the Mississippi a few cyards from the road.

"Aren't there any closing laws in Plaquemine Parish?"

"Only two laws here," the stranger smiled, "the church and Leander Perez."

The lights and music had awakened Jake, and he heard the name Perez.

"They say he runs Plaquemine stronger'n George Parr handles Duval County. Remember when the federal government wanted to send in disaster relief after that hurricane, and old Perez wired the President he'd just as soon take care of the needy in Plaquemine Parish? And he did, too."

"Yeah," said Mickey, "it's a different world, and let's try and not forget that."

They hit Venice at daybreak, strained the boat lift at Elzee's Marina with the heavy Formula, and cruised out into the swirling brown current of the Mississippi.

Barges, towboats, ships, seaplanes dipping low over the river, nothing seemed to catch the attention of the stranger. In the light of day, he was dark, obviously old, yet with remarkably few lines or creases; a face of strange serenity.

They were taking on fuel at Port Eads when the Cajun on the dock casually remarked that there was no bait today; the light plant had gone off, and the frozen mullet and balao had spoiled.

Jake's jaw dropped; Mickey slammed the cleaning rag against the deck.

The stranger raised his hand, and motioned toward the Gulf. "There will be bait," he said.

At the mouth of the river, Jake flipped the radio to 2182, and called the Coast Guard.

A young voice answered and advised him to stay on that frequency, and to call in occasionally, because they were the only sport boat offshore.

As they cleared the tiny jetties and felt the boat come alive with the roll of the Gulf, the stranger pointed off to port and Jake complied with the wheel, picking up the distant speck of an oil rig on the horizon.

Mickey pointed to another speck near the rig. "Coast Guard was wrong," he said. "There's at least one other boat out here."

They pulled nearer and made out the classic, ageless lines of a high-sided dory, bobbing like a white cork in the green waves, two men in it and both with light rods bending under a swarm of feeding gulls.

"Go nearer," the stranger said. "They have mackerel."

"We'll foul up their action," Jake protested.

The stranger shook his head and Jake found himself turning the wheel, wondering who was in charge of his boat.

The men were dark, same as the stranger, and exchanged a few words so rapidly Jake wasn't prepared when the first mackerel came flying through the air and hit the deck. They threw in half a dozen, all small forktails just the right size for marlin.

When Jake reached into his pocket, one of them shook his head, smiled, and cast out again, turning his back on them.

Jake turned toward the open Gulf, and suddenly felt the stranger's hand over his, pulling back on the throttles.

"First," he said, head bowing, "let us pray."

Jake threw a quick look at Mickey, shrugged, and bowed his head.

The prayer must have been in Cajun because neither of them could understand it, but it was short, and the man straightened up, smiled, and motioned offshore. Jake hit the throttles, the Formula cleared herself of one wave and mushed into the next, and within fifteen minutes they crossed the clearly drawn line between green water and the indigo blue of the deep Gulf. Just offshore were the first patches of floating sargassum weed, the famous South Pass "rip" where mighty Gulf currents meet and debris from the sea and the Mississippi form wide, floating avenues of shade and cover for baitfish and dolphin, lanes which big wahoo, marlin, sail, and tuna prowl relentlessly, waiting for smaller fish to leave the protection of the grass.

With both outriggers up, two fresh mackerel bouncing from wave to wave on the surface, and a yellow feather jig on the flatline in the wake of the engines, Jake turned closer to the line of floating grass, then paralleled it. Almost instantly there was a streak of green and blue, and a magnificent bull dolphin was clear of the water with the yellow feather jig in his jaw.

Jake scrambled to get the outrigger baits out of Mickey's way, and as he yanked the starboard line out of the outrigger pin and began cranking up fast, the bait surfaced and below it was a giant, dark shadow. A bill the size of a baseball bat came out of a wave and a geyser of water exploded into foam as the 10/0 Penn screamed off line against the clicker.

"My God," yelled Mickey, "there's a marlin after my dolphin!"

"Your dolphin, hell," Jake gritted, "he's got my mackerel." The screaming reel picked up speed, and he lowered the rod tip, braced both feet, and threw the gear handle forward. Instantly the lurch of tremendous power yanked him to the stern, colliding him bodily with Mickey, and then simultaneously two magnificent blue marlin cleared the surface, as perfectly as porpoises from the same school, greyhounding side by side. A doubleheader on blue marlin!

"Woweeee," Jake Rebel-yelled, "keep that yearlin' out of my way!"

"Mine's gut-hooked and bleeding," Mickey groaned, watching line disappear from the reel. "If we get a school of sharks up here we could lose 'em both."

An hour later, both men were sodden with sweat, pumping and cranking, taking turns using the single fighting chair, both in kidney harnesses and gaining line.

"Shark!" Mickey yelled, as his fish suddenly shot clear of the surface with a brownish shadow beneath him.

Suddenly the water was alive with sharks, circling fast, moving in for the kill. The stranger quickly threw over two peculiar rigs he'd put together, a few feet of wire leader with a hook on one end and a buoyant boat fender on the other. They went bobbing behind the boat, baited with whole mackerel, and instantly a shark had each mackerel with the moving fenders disappearing, only to reappear, bobbing uncertainly. Other sharks swarmed around the hooked ones, attacking the white boat fenders, trying to get in on the feast. A ripped, bloody head of a mackerel floated up for an instant, was engulfed by a blue-gray brute with two others on his tail, and then the whole seething exploding procession was moving off from the boat, decoying every shark in the school with them.

"Now that was some trick," Jake said in awe.

"Yeah," grunted Mickey, "but did you ever stop to think of the next little problem, such as how to get two three-hundred-plus marlin into one 23-foot boat without a gin pole?"

The stranger was up forward, fiddling with the radio, and suddenly a voice broke in through the static. "This is the *Seabird* back to the boat calling."

The motor noise was too much for them to hear the stranger's conversation, but the *Seabird* came back again, loud and clear. "We should be there within thirty minutes; we'll bring an extra flying gaff. Now give me a long, slow count, to get a fix on you."

"Well, I'll be damned," said Mickey. "He's done it again. I never thought about calling one of those charter boats back at Port Eads for help; he must know the guy or something."

Both marlin were whipped, unable to sound, but still deeper than the fifteen-foot cable leader, indistinct, blue forms below the boat, when the 46-foot *Seabird* pulled alongside. The mate jumped aboard to help with the flying gaff, and after half an hour of grunting, groaning, flying spray and one marlin bill ramming into the planked hull of the *Seabird* . . . it was all over. Two giant fish were on the *Seabird*'s decks, both over three hundred pounds, colors starting to fade from the angry, neon blue of fighting marlin into the gunmetal gray of vanquished trophies.

At the Port Eads docks, people swarmed around the hanging fish, asking questions and taking pictures, and in the confusion the little stranger disappeared.

"Maybe he caught a ride back to Venice with some other boat," Jake pondered. "But he wouldn't leave without us paying him, would he?"

At dusk they gave up looking and headed upriver, bucking the current and watching for floating logs, and at Elzee's Marina, nobody even remembered seeing the quiet stranger with them. Nor had anyone seen a white New England dory, nor any two men with a catch of mackerel.

That night in the motel café, Jake inquired further about the stranger.

"Dunno," the waitress pondered. "Lot of strange people around here lately, foreigners. You know they're having that big deal over in the Vatican about liberalizing the church and all, and Mr. Perez is about the most important Catholic in all of Louisiana. I guess they figure the way he decides is the way we'll all go."

That night in bed, listening to ship foghorns on the river and sipping scotch in the darkness, Jake wrestled with reason.

"That dory we saw out there, you remember the numbers on her?"

Mickey groaned, "There were no numbers. And the Coast Guard told us we were the only boat out! Jake, who the devil did we have out in that boat with us?"

Jake sat straight up in bed. "Please," he said, "do me a favor. Don't even say the word 'devil' again until we get out of Plaquemine Parish. And tomorrow, you and me are going to Mass for the first time in our lives!"

Of Perches and Pleasures

The warmth of early spring sun was transfusing fresh, saffron life into the greening willows, and the redwing blackbirds and bull-frogs set up a coarse chorus in the upper end of the old oxbow lake which once had been the channel of the Trinity River.

Uncle William idled along the shoreline with a freshly cut elm stick for a walking cane, and somewhere within those cav-ernous blue overalls I knew there was a crappie line wrapped around a quill float made from the wing feather of a wild goose.

But he still had not admitted we were going fishing. If the "signs" were not right, he threatened to work on his back fence.

The old cypress skiff, bottom up and covered with leaves, was hidden in a pile of logs beside the water, and when I reached down to turn it over he stopped me and shook his head sadly.

"Jess ain't no hope fo' you, is theah? Now how many times Ah tole you to look befo' you steps; cain't you see dat cottonmouf moccasin under dat boat?"

I jumped back instinctively and shuddered as he killed the black foul-smelling snake with one well-placed blow with the stick.

"Lucky you had that stick with you."

"Lucky," he snorted. "How come you think Ah tote dat stick all de way over heah? They's allus due to be at least one snake under a laid-up boat, an' you don't know dat neither?"

He frowned further when I began putting together the featherlight little three-piece tubular steel flyrod. "An' speakin' o' dat, I jess as soon see a snake come swimmin' up heah wid one gold tooth as to have one o' dem things whippin' 'round mah eahs."

"What's wrong with a flyrod? All the magazines say they're the sportiest way to fish."

"Nobody say nothin' 'bout spoaht; yeahs ago Ah guided a feller whuppin one o' dem things; he liketa put mah eyes out wid it. But least he had one made outa cane, dat wouldn't draw lightnin' like dat thing you got."

The sky rumbled as if to punctuate his pronouncement, and I put up the flyrod. No use to cross Uncle William nor the lightning.

The lake was long and narrow, as the river had been, with button willows lining the shorelines and enough green willows to provide Uncle William with a few new brushpiles every year.

He was very careful about cutting his "perch trees" in such a way that the brushy top of the tree would fall well out from shore, in deep water, and he never cut all the way through the trunk, just enough so he could shove it over and leave the trunk attached to the stump where it couldn't move around out of place if the water rose.

I realized why he took such pains when he pulled up to a brush top he'd cut two weeks before.

"What are those two white cords hanging down off the brush?"

"Well, one o' 'em is a minner jar wid some corn meal an' most likely some redhorses in it," he grunted, "an' de other is jess in case one o' dem snakes do git us."

He hauled up the latter cord with utmost care and six brown bottles of homebrewed beer, cooled from the very bottom of the lake, clanked invitingly as he slipped one of them off the string and let it down again.

He opened the bottle with his teeth, as he always did, and the cap blew off with a powerful report and a cloud of foam. His brew had been known to go off by itself on a hot day, and he handled it with the tender loving care of a hand grenade.

"Now in case you an' youah runnin' buddy Richard jess might happen along by dis row o' bresh tops widout me, Ah know better'n to tell y'all to leave dis beah alone. But jess in case dat should happen, don't try an' do what I jess done, because white folks' teeth ain't made fo' it, an' also because I seen a yeller nigger from over across de river try dat one time wid some o' my brew an' de cap blowed off an' fired rat down his throat. He was plumb purple befo' I could cut me a stick an' shove it on down."

"You mean you just shoved a bottle cap down in a man's stomach? What did it do to his insides?"

Uncle William took a long, savoring sip, and his belly shook in silent laughter.

"Don't know 'bout dat but he still live over yonder, an' dey says he never been troubled wid piles since."

The big-mouthed Ball jar he was pulling through the greenish water was flashing and swarming full of minnows, half obscured in the stirred-up white cornmeal, and he dumped the whole mess into the rusty minnow bucket that he kept along with the cane poles under the boat. The minnow jar was a crude sort

of trap, a cone of screen wire with the small end of the cone inside the jar. A minnow would be funneled naturally into the tiny
opening just big enough for him to enter, but his odds of hitting
such a small hole from the other way were practically nil, because
the little fish kept bumping the sides of the jar rather than trying
to go out the middle.

Uncle William took a strong, struggling redhorse with
bright-pink fins and inserted the light crappie hook just behind
the dorsal fin. Then he carefully pushed the point of the hook
back into the minnow's side to hide it.

He set the goose-quill float about four feet deep, and let the
minnow carefully down through an opening in the still-green
willow leaves. The quill, with only a dime with a hole in it for
weight, sat up perfectly straight and bobbed lightly with the

swimming minnow below. Suddenly it bobbed under, came back up, and lay over on its side.

Uncle William grunted, raised the light cane pole slowly but firmly, and it bent and whipped with the circling fight of a big white crappie. I caught a green willow limb.

We made three more brushpiles, each containing a fresh, cool brew for Uncle William, and also a number of crappie, and I could stand the licking no longer.

"I'm doing something wrong, and you're not telling me what it is."

"Up to now, you ain't asked."

"OK, I give up; I get hung and you go down right beside me and come up with a saddleblanket perch, how come?"

"Well, fo' one thing you leaves de pint o' de hook showin' an' fo' another you ain't got no dime fo' a weight, an' fo' another you ain't much of a white perch fisherman."

"It's more'n that," I argued. "No perch can see whether that hook is covered down deep in this water; I've swum down deep and opened my eyes and it's nothin' but dark down there. And I don't see it does any more good havin' that dime for a weight than it does for you to wear that dime around your right leg on a string, which is nothing but superstition and you know it."

Uncle William pondered the brash outburst as he always did, sorrowfully but with patience.

"Thass right," he sighed, "but how many you ketch today? If you must know, buryin' dat hook pint in de minner ain't to hide it from him, an' dat dime ain't necessarily jess fo' weight. You ever hear of a spinner, boy? Dat dime jess de right weight fo' dat quill, which you also ain't got, an' it so light dat when a perch suck dat minner in his mouf, he don't feel no big stopper-cork lak you got, nor no big weight, an' he don't feel dat minner bite back at him wid de pint o' dat hook, neither. An' if you won-derin' how come you gets hung, it's dat you jerk an' don't work around an' lift up easy, an' because de pint of dat hook is jess lookin' fo' a limb to stick."

Midway of the lecture his quill had suddenly darted out of

sight, and this time it just kept going. Instantly he reached back
with the paddle and began pulling out into the open water, the
cane pole lurching and jerking.

"Ah thought you ought to be 'long heah somewheah," he
muttered to the fish, spitting a dark stream of snuff in his excitement. "Der always least one trout o' two right along dis deep
bank."

Uncle William persisted in calling a bass a trout, for the
same reason he called a bowfin a grinner and a greenhead a
mallet.

"Easy der," he said, coaxing the fish in the same tone he
used on the mules, "thass right, you jess come by heah one mo'
time like dat."

Suddenly his right hand darted down to the water and came
up with a four-pound bass gripped just behind the gills, tail curling and as if paralyzed by the grip.

"All the magazines say to grip a bass by the lower lip to boat
him," I informed.

"Dat so," he mused, careful to work the light hook out without bending it. "Youah magazines ever see a fish hawk dive an'
ketch a fish? Well, wheah do he ketch him, in de lip o' behind de
head? 'Course now, no fish hawk know nothin' 'bout ketching a
fish, like dem magazines do."

We had one more brush top to go, and it was just as well because Uncle William's homebrew was always put up with a small
chunk of raw potato in the bottom of each bottle, which by con-
tinuing the fermentation after bottling, produced a potion of
power and proof permitting only a limited number of brush tops
per fishing trip.

A flight of gadwalls passed over high, lowered flaps, and disappeared behind the trees, followed by two more flights in rapid
succession. They were obviously going to roost on the river, big
ducks on their way back north for the mating season, fat from
wintering in the rice fields. It would be easy to stalk them from
the high bluff bank, and Uncle William's big double-barreled
shotgun was in the wagon.

"Don't even mention it," he warned. "We done had it out

befo' 'bout de duck laws. Der ain't no duck shootin' in de penitentiary, an' dat's wheah you headed if'n you don' change yo ways. What is you gonna be when you grows up?" he mumbled around the underlip permanently pooched with Garrett's Snuff. "You sho don't take to no work 'round heah!"

"Be a book writer and travel all over the world and catch great big fish like Mr. Zane Grey."

He pulled up the little quill, let the minnow wiggle in the air, and dropped it over into another opening in the willow top.

"What kinna fish do he ketch?"

"Oh, monster fish. I don't know all the names, but I've seen pictures, fish as big as Rodney, fish as big as any mule you ever saw. Ocean fish."

Uncle William frowned and spat a darker brown into the water.

"Ain't no fish big as Rodney, an' he ain't much mule. An' if you gonna be a book writer, how come you ain't in school to-day?"

When he laughed he did it inside, but you could tell because his belly would be shaking inside his overalls, and his eyes would be watering if he was really tickled.

"What you gonna do wid dat monster ocean fish when you ketches him? You sho cain't eat him, an' you cain't string him, an' you gonna be so wore out when you ketches dat mule fish, you cain't even drag him home."

He was shaking like that inside the overalls all the way up the bank, belly bobbing, thinking about that fish as big as old Rodney.

"Thass bound to be what you gonna be, boy, a book writer, 'cause you sho got what it take to be a book writer; you is, in fact, jess plumb full o' it!"

A Small Wager
Among Gentlemen

The country between Corpus Christi and Kingsville was hot and dry, parched soil baking under a sun as merciless in October as August, mesquite brush along Highway 77 dusty and drawn, as if the plants had pulled in all vital juices to survive until rain.

Even in the air-conditioned car, the three men in the back seat were uncomfortable, possibly because their clothing had not been designed for Texas on the opening day of South Zone dove season.

The man in front beside the Mexican driver was sipping a cold beer, eyes darting like black beetles behind heavy horn-rimmed glasses.

"Now let's go through this one more time; there can be no foulups, no mistakes. You guys are just old friends of mine, and we've hunted together for years. Grouse hunted, ruffed grouse, great bird. Okay? Now you don't know a thing about the bet. If the Colonel brings it up, fine, but act surprised. The Colonel's no fool."

Morgan Winters took another sip of beer, adjusted his glasses, and turned to watch the countryside. It had been a long time, but the shimmering heat haze over the brush country had not changed. He hated the country; he'd had to grow up in it, been humiliated in it, rolled in the dust of it by boys and bulls, and by his uncle, the Colonel. But there was money in this dust and cactus, and he'd left with his share the minute he was twenty-one. Now he was coming back for more.

South of Kingsville, with the sun lower and shadows lengthening across the road, they began seeing doves. The men in the back seat leaned forward and watched the streamlined gray dots hurtling over the mesquite.

"Jeez, they're fast little guys, ain't they?" the short one observed. "Maybe I should'a brought shorter, open barrels."

"Marty, you quit talking like that. You tell ole Morgan you got exactly the right gun or I'll call this deal off right now; we're shootin' for big potatoes, boy, and these guys out here are not all clod farmers."

Marty grinned. "You just leave the shootin' to us and you get the bets on."

It had taken Morgan a while to pick his crew; two were Eastern Zone skeet champions, the third had just set a new record at the Grand American Trapshoot. All were young, cool, and liked money. The real gamble wasn't in the shooting at all, but in whether any of these ranch folk he remembered as being so isolated from the rest of the world just happened to be keeping up with trap or skeet lately.

The gate into the ranch was exactly as he remembered, and

so was the dusty gravel road which wound on and on through the brush country past sleek, reddish Santa Gertrudis steers huddled under the meager shade of mesquites. Two Mexicans on horseback in leather chaps and sweat-stained straw hats turned out of the ruts as they passed a windmill pond, exactly the sort of place they would be hunting.

Morgan told the driver to stop, and they got out and walked over to the windmill.

"Take a good look at this setup," Morgan instructed. "These doves come in fast, often they'll dive right in over the mesquite, and if you try and take 'em then, you'll overshoot. Wait until they flare and start off again. Any of you guys ever shoot doves before?"

Marty laughed. "Where I come from," he said, "little things like that are called songbirds."

The winding gravel drive up to the ranchhouse was an abrupt change from drought to oasis, verdant green carpetgrass and shrubbery with the air cool and moist from whirling sprinklers, the rambling Spanish house all but obscured by blooming bougainvillea.

The Colonel was putting on his usual fiesta for the opening of hunting season, and music was coming from the patio. Other guests strolled the green lawns with tinkling drinks in hand, enjoying the cool of evening.

Two white-jacketed Mexican boys appeared, and behind them, the tall imposing figure of the Colonel. He had changed little in the twenty years since Morgan had seen him, the same high boots, bushy mustache, and impeccable crease to the Western dress suit, an imposing man not so much in height as in stature.

"I see you brought your grouse-shooting friends," the Colonel said significantly, shaking Morgan's hand first. "Delightful, and welcome back to the ranch!"

He shook hands with each of them in turn, a remarkably firm grip for a man crowding seventy, and ushered them into the patio where the mariachi band was playing and the drinks were being served by a white-haired Negro who had been with the

Colonel since Pancho Villa was occasionally making raids along the border.

After dinner, when the ladies had retired to the veranda and the men were smoking on the patio, the Colonel proposed a toast to one of the locals, a white-templed rancher in tall snakeproof boots, for winning the "Laredo Shoot."

"What is a Laredo Shoot?" John Saxton whispered to Morgan.

"Probably some sort of local game they have around here; I remember they used to have a trap set up right behind the ranch house to throw in all directions, a homemade deal you guys could eat up like apple pie."

The next morning everyone slept late, there was coffee about ten, and the shooting guests from neighboring ranches began arriving nearer noon.

Morgan was getting restless because the Colonel had surprised him already. First, he had feared there would be only a token bet, and he'd had to pay his hired guns two hundred apiece, plus air fare. Now, the Colonel was needling about his young Yankees coming down to fleece the country boys, but offering to bet five thousand dollars. Also, the Colonel wanted an observer for every pair of shooters, and the rules were that if the observer ruled a bird within range, the shooter had to take the shot. The winners would be the shooters who took the birds as they came, and got their twelve-bird limits with the fewest shells.

But as the gunners gathered to be assigned vehicles and guides, the lure of the five thousand became stronger. In daylight the Colonel's men looked older, and they were already drinking beer while his men sipped Cokes, young pros against aging amateurs, Cokes against Carta Blanca . . . and he was worried?

He walked over to the Colonel, stuck out his hand, and the bet was on.

At three o'clock the caravan formed, the Colonel and Morgan driving to the largest waterhole, where Saxton and Marty would shoot against two ranchers, Gus Price and Bruce Richardson. Mark Wright had been paired with a neighboring rancher named Sanchez, and they would shoot on a small windmill tank not far away.

Sitting in the shade of the Colonel's custom-built hunting car, which had once been a Mercury convertible, Morgan sipped a beer and prepared for the slaughter. It was more than the five thousand to him.

The doves began flying, high and with the wind; and the observers on the big tank, a couple of the Colonel's doctor friends from Corpus Christi, called no shots even though a few might have been in range.

Then a flight of half a dozen appeared low over the mesquite, heading straight for the waterhole, and both observers called "birds!" almost simultaneously.

They came hurtling with the wind, suddenly cupping wings and losing altitude, and Saxton and Marty waited coolly, remembering Morgan's warning. The lead dove exploded as if hit with a hand grenade.

Morgan jumped out of the hunting car and screamed, "God-dammit, you both shot the same bird," but his words were lost in the roar of gunfire from the Texas end of the tank; Price and Richardson had methodically, almost slowly, collapsed four birds in sequence.

They were reloading the two battered over-unders when the next flight pitched in over Marty and Saxton. This time with signals clear, Saxton showed a brilliant flash of handling speed, dumping both his birds, two shots from the skeet-bored Remington automatic blending almost into one.

Saxton rolled his first bird beautifully, the other dived toward the ground after his falling partner, and the second shot raked feathers from his back as he disappeared over the mesquite.

Over on the windmill tank, Mark Wright was assaying his problem. The doves were coming in head-on and losing altitude, which meant the first shot had to be watched carefully to avoid overshooting, and the second would be almost directly overhead.

The Texan had the first chance at a pair which seemed almost out of range, but the observer called the shot and he killed one and missed one.

To a trapshooter, that one bird lost could mean the match. Wright relaxed, smiled to himself, and watched three little dots dipping and swerving, coming straight for the windmill.

"Birds!" yelled the observer. Wright brought up the high-stocked Model 12 pump; the lead dove exploded into a mangled mass of feathers from the tight full choke, and he turned to take the second. More white feathers floated in the air, but the two birds were still dipping and diving.

He couldn't believe it! He'd shot behind, and he'd led that bird three feet!

At the big waterhole, Morgan was standing beside the hunting car, eyes narrowed, and the Colonel had walked around the back to pull a cold Carta Blanca.

"Ah still don't see," he drawled with an exaggerated accent, "how the Yankees evah won the war."

The doves were whipping in from all angles, hearing the gunfire and circling before piling in, and the Texans were watching their erratic, diving swerves and turns, waiting for the split second of commitment, and firing in that instant.

It looked easy, but Marty had missed four straight, and Saxton was feathering birds, hitting too far back, losing them in the brush.

Price had a beer to his lips when a single came hurtling in from behind. The observer called the bird, and Price whirled and killed him with the 12-gauge cradled across the crook of one arm.

"Use both hands now, Gus," the Colonel bellowed, brownish mustache quivering with mirth. "Let's be gentlemen about this."

Back at the ranch that night, with the packet of bills exchanged and four fingers of straight bourbon beginning to take out some of the sting, Morgan leveled.

"I've never seen shooting like that in my life," he mused. "I'll tell you where I got my boys if you'll tell me where you got yours."

"Right around here," the Colonel smiled. "That is, if you consider Amarillo, Wichita Falls, and McAllen right around here. You see, we have a little local game around Texas and Louisiana which I understand may even be spreading into your country. It's called Colombaire pigeons, originated in Spain, you know, live birds thrown by a professional thrower or *colombaire*. The boys you were betting against shoot almost every weekend someplace; Price just took the International Championships at Laredo. I really do believe they're among the finest shotgun shots in the world today."

Marty, who had been listening, got up and stomped out heavily across the Mexican tile.

"We didn't have the right guns this time, and it was new to us," he said. "But we'll be back."

"By all means," the Colonel said graciously. "You're welcome at the ranch any time.

"And by the way," he added, glancing at Morgan, "please bring money. As you know, that's about the only way we have of keeping this miserable country green."

The Canvasback Jury

It would be, he admitted, a rather ugly place to die. The drab Louisiana marsh stretched away into a hazy infinity of cane islands, moated by sulphurous bogs into which a man would flounder and sink to his armpits in one step.

With the bitter north wind blowing, he would die of exposure, he figured, within eight hours.

Eight hours . . . he breathed heavily from the exertion, poling the tiny bateau to the hard ground of the island. Red, the aging Chesapeake retriever, jumped overboard and splashed through the bog for the last few steps to the island, nosing around for the crippled duck he expected to be there. Why else would the old man leave the blind and pole over to the little island?

The bateau slid up into an inlet, and man and dog waded ashore.

"Suicide." He snorted at the thought. "The worst, most ridiculous word. The stupid word. This may be stupid, but it's not exactly that word."

He sat down heavily on a hummock of grass and felt the north wind bite suddenly through the heavy canvas coat.

"Well, why does a man do anything? Why does he kill himself to make money, or risk his life to buy a pretty girl pretty things?"

He looked down at his legs, muddy and encased in the ridiculously clumsy waders. They were long legs, still strong. He had been a good man, a powerful man.

He struggled to his feet, clumsy in the waders, and realized the sun was sinking behind the cane.

"I've got to know," he said aloud to the dog. "Is that crazy to you, Red, that I have to know . . . and this is the only chance I would ever have. You've got to realize that; deep down every man wonders about his woman, but most are cowards who never find out."

He thought about the dog. Red would live. He had the fur and the ancestry to live. He would be there when they came. He would be sad, if a dog can be sad, but alive.

Deliberately he sloshed through the edge of the muck and shoved the bateau away from the island. It floated idly across the shallow water, then, caught by the wind, swiftly raced into the channel, another leaf scudding ahead of the wind, then a tiny gray speck in the marsh.

For an instant, terror gripped him, strange because fear was a stranger. "It is," he laughed to himself, "a little late to get scared."

A flight of canvasbacks came whistling downwind, crossed the open water, and came back against the norther, looking for the scant protection of the tiny island. He watched them, the strongest, fastest, largest of all ducks . . . this was their weather; they like it rough. All the other ducks were far back in the sheltered cane, or in the coves in the lee of the wind. But the big, white-breasted cans were flying.

The big dog whined softly as the ducks whipped overhead almost near enough to touch and alighted upwind, beating their wings and preening themselves in the gale as if nothing was happening. It was fitting, he thought, the toughest ducks and a tough, hardheaded old man sitting it out together. If this was to be a trial, they would be the only jury to witness it.

Across the water he could see the eerie, flickering light of the big flare beside the first well he had drilled in this country. It had been a great one, and it had, along with the field which came behind it, made him millions.

Someday there would be no more flares; men like himself had to be tough, to get what they could, and waste much in the process. But man was needing his resources more now; they would find ways to channel that hissing gas elsewhere; there would be no such waste, and no such flares.

But he was glad this one was still there. It was all he had now of civilization, and it would also be a good navigational aid to Jacques if he did come in the big boat. Jacques would know where to look, if he wanted to know; the deep channel to the well passed beside the island.

He had overheard his wife talking with the good-looking young roughneck he had picked out of the oil fields to run his hunting club, a Cajun same as she was, from the country where he'd found her. He knew she had been having an affair with Jacques. It had started at the first of waterfowl season, perhaps the first time she saw him. It was obvious, and it was easy to understand. At seventy no man can keep a woman like Yvette from looking at handsome men.

The cook had overheard their plans. She was leaving him tomorrow night, a Saturday (why do all Cajuns have to do big things on Saturday night, like get married, drunk or run away . . .).

Yvette didn't need him any more. She had her part of the

estate, or would in any divorce, or maybe she had been slipping away some money all these years . . . the way she spent money she could have stashed a fortune in five years.

It had to come. He had seen it coming with his age.

But it was important if she had ever loved him, way back then, or if he'd been a blind fool all those years.

When he did not return to the club, it would be easy for Jacques to search in the wrong places. There was no one to know better except Yvette. And it was a very big marsh.

It would be simple. If Yvette did not demand that Jacques come to search in the right places, then they would be very rich indeed. The will had been long since signed and sealed. She knew what was in it.

This would be the easy way for them. And he knew how Yvette could rationalize . . . after all, he was old. He did not have

long . . . and he had had a very big life, with plenty of women in the first half and plenty of money in the last. "He had his life," she would say, "and so now we can have ours, Jacques. He will have died the way he liked to live, with his dog, hunting in the marsh . . ."

It wouldn't be very difficult to convince Jacques. Jacques had the morals of a mink. Maybe, he grinned to himself, Jacques could do things like a mink.

With the loss of the sun, the cold came swiftly, first the pain of face and feet. He took off his gloves, rubbed his hands. Then they went numb.

He looked at the big diamond ring and smiled to himself. He'd always thought of it as a sort of symbol of himself, a bright, burning-white diamond, with strength and vigor of love of life . . . he had swapped half-interest in a well in South Africa for that ring . . . when he was drunk and very young.

He remembered the night in Caracas when the ring had so badly carved the face of a man in Los Cocos bar that he had been forced to buy the place, bar and bartender, to stay out of jail. And all the women who wanted to wear that ring . . . and one who had worn it for a night, around her neck, on the same chain with her crucifix, a gleaming white diamond between the dark, Latin breasts.

Red, the dog, snuggled against him, shivering. The north wind had increased, howling in the cane, and somewhere a nutria screamed its odd, almost human wail of mating ecstasy . . .

"They pick cold, wet places to make love, don't they, Red." He snuggled against the warmth of the dog. "Like old men pick cold, wet places to learn if they have been . . ."

He buttoned his jacket to the top, and turned up the collar.

His thoughts drifted to other women. Why had they not made him wonder about love? Such as Eva, in Buenos Aires, when he was young . . . he wondered what became of her . . . God, what a woman. He remembered how she clung to him the night he left, holding to him as he tried to leave the room, sliding to the floor and crying and holding to his legs . . .

"Probably married and dumpy, with seven little brown brats around the house," he said to the dog.

"How is it that there always seems to be some fool who turns up and moves in, believing whatever they say . . . always some dullard she can turn to after the big thrill is gone, to keep her company and sire her children, and listen to her tell him how she's never felt this way about a man before . . ."

He thought of Yvette, soft and warm in bed beside him, how it had been the nights in the mountains, in the big cabin, when she was still young and wide-eyed at things like money, and rich things, and the man who had them . . . maybe those things she said, the little things she did, maybe they were real then . . . he argued with himself.

"She was what you wanted. You bought her and you paid the price. She did her end of the bargain well . . . so very well," he smiled into the wind, feeling a stirring where a man of seventy is supposed to feel few stirrings.

He lit a cigarette and looked at his watch. He'd know soon. If they were coming, they would come within two hours after dark . . . he shuddered . . . those last four hours would be bad. He would know the answer, and there would be nothing left but to face it, no hope. He realized with a flush of warmth, there was still some hope.

The canvasbacks swam in closer to the island. He had thirty more minutes to hope. The night was black, and the world had shrunk into a dog and a man and two canvasbacks in the lee of the island, two dots on the dark water.

He could not feel his feet, nor his nose, but his legs began to cramp from the position, and he wondered if he could move them . . .

But his mind was not numb. With the cold, it grew sharper. He tried to think of himself, to see himself with the eyes of some distant observer . . .

"He was gray, and she always noticed dark men, like herself. His body was not very handsome even when he met her. He never let her see much of his body in the light, and he never swam with her or sunbathed with her.

"But how had his body felt to her in the dark . . . compared to the strong, young arms of the young men whom she'd danced and skied and swum with . . . ?"

When a man is a happy fool, he cannot think of how he must look in the early mornings, a haggard old man with bags beneath his eyes, ugly and snoring . . . he shuddered.

"How," he wondered, "can a man make himself believe what he wants to believe?"

He was asleep when they found him. He had heard the chugging of the diesel shrimp boat Jacques used, but he dreamed it was the old steam rig of his first well in Venezuela, chugging softly in the jungle. He was dreaming of the heat of the jungle.

He did not awake until Jacques was carrying him, his head bouncing against the coarse canvas jacket, and he pretended to be asleep as Yvette piled gunny sacks, her own coat and Jacques' jacket in heaps upon him. She was speaking to him as she had when she was excited, some of the words and phrases she had said in bed when she was in ecstasy . . . he remembered the phrases, and a new warmth began spreading over him. She had indeed meant them then.

At the big fireplace in the lodge, with a steaming coffee laced with brandy, his feet and hands ached terribly, but he had long since learned to control pain. Pain is something a man can fight.

He had slipped the big, white ring on her finger, made the speech short and simple, and told them to go, and the ring had sparkled with a new light as if new, young life had flowed into it.

He turned to the fire, and long after the chugging of the boat was lost in the howl of the chimney and crackling of the fire . . . he stepped outside and opened the door against the gale.

"It's all right now, Red," he said. "You can come in now."

The Sharks

The line of blue water which had been hanging offshore beyond the breakers was moving almost within casting range with the incoming tide, and Earl Garrigus stood on the porch of the unpainted shack and watched it through his binoculars.

"Time we get there, it'll be clear to the beach," he observed. "Good many birds startin' to work over toward the pass."

Neal Martin poured two fingers of bourbon, reached for

more ice, and looked at his watch. He could fish until six and still
have time to get back home in time to meet the Winstons.

"You guys look out for sharks, now," Felix Stephens said,
sticking his head out of the kitchen, where he was cooking up a
crab gumbo. "If there's anything to that radio report a while ago,
we could have the same deal they had down at Port Isabel yesterday."

Neal shuddered. A Brownsville wade fisherman had died
from loss of blood after a shark attack in the surf near Port Isabel.
And according to the commentator, a number of other sightings
of big sharks had been made in the surf, due to a rare inward shift
of Gulf currents which had brought deep Gulf water almost in to
the beach.

"Aw, Felix, hell," Earl griped, "you believe everything you
hear?"

"Why would anybody make up a story like that?"

"I don't doubt the man got hit," Earl argued, "but how
many years have we fished the San Luis Pass surf, and how many
people ever got hurt by a shark? I can't think of one."

"Lot of people have disappeared around that pass," Felix
countered, "and who knows what's happened to 'em? If those big
offshore sharks followed the blue water in, it could be reasonable
that one of 'em would hit a man's leg, particularly if he happened
to have a stringer of fish wrapped around it."

"Bull," Earl said, reaching for his fishing rod leaning against
the cabin. "A shark is a shark."

Galveston Island was green and blooming with spring, and
yellow-breasted meadowlarks jumped and flew ahead of the dune
buggy as they crossed over to the surf.

"Man, it's good to be away from town," Neal said, stretching in the sunshine. "Seems every time I try to get off, something
else comes up. You know how it is."

"No, I don't," said Earl. "I fish three times a week."

They waded in slowly, casting into the first gut of the surf,
then crossing the waist-deep second gut, and tiptoeing up to their
necks to find the hard ridge of the third bar underfoot.

The incoming waves hissed and boomed, breaking behind

them, and as each wall of water steepened before curling into foam Neal could see through the translucent tops as if they were glass.

"You ever see the surf like this in your life?" he yelled between waves.

Earl shook his head and made a long, low cast, his silver spoon glinting in the afternoon sun and disappearing behind the steepening crest of the next wave.

A flock of birds began moving toward them, dipping and squealing in their feeding, and as a particularly big wave curled over Neal saw dark shapes in it, backlit by the afternoon sun.

"Surf's full of mullet," Earl yelled. "Got to be fish here."

Neal caught a strong whiff of watermelon, the unmistakable smell of feeding fish. Earl pointed with his rod to the big, spreading oil slick on the surface just beyond casting distance.

"Now that's damn sure trout," he yelled, "can you reach 'em?"

Neal tried to throw farther and backlashed. Earl's spoon, with less wind resistance, made it almost to the slick and dropped into a trough. Instantly a silver flash came streaking down a wave and his rod arched and lurched.

Neal's trembling fingers picked at the backlash, a wave broke in his face and almost knocked him down, and as he cranked back in fast for another cast the rod suddenly leaped in his hands.

Clumsily he fought the fish, realizing how long it had been, turning his back to the waves and trying to get the flopping, darting streak of silver safely pinned against his leg without hooking himself.

Earl had put three on the stringer by that time, lean, sea-run specks with brilliant black dots on their tails and fins.

For an hour they caught trout, and Neal forgot for the first time in a long time about his watch, the Winstons, and even his wife.

He was starting to make a cast when he heard Earl yell, and it was a sort of sound he had never heard from those hardbitten old lips.

When he looked there was only a straw hat full of lures floating, and then a wave crashed past and Earl was struggling to come up out of the water but being yanked back down again.

Terror gripped Neal as he saw the huge, dark shape in the clear water. He tried to run, almost fell, got going again until the shape was almost at his feet, beating the water frantically with his rod with one hand and trying to help Earl up with the other.

Breaking waves thundered around them, and Earl was being dragged backward by his stringer. Neal groped for the heavy cord, felt it, and yanked upward with all his might. The water exploded with another wave, and as it passed he could see the shark's gaping mouth, the stringer of trout hanging out of it, the ugly snout shaking and tearing at the fish.

He felt the stringer pull loose from Earl, and dragged him to his feet, yelling and beating the water and cursing the shark.

Suddenly something had his leg; he panicked, then realized it was his own stringer; he was wrapped in it, and the crashing

waves tangled it around him. Frantically he fought to free himself, hauled up on the stringer to pull it loose, and in that instant a blue-gray streak came from nowhere and the water surged and boiled around their legs.

"Run," Earl was yelling, "there's a school of the big bastards."

They made the last few yards through the shallow water, and never stopped until they got to the beach buggy. Neal found the plastic flask of bourbon on the floorboard and each drank half of it at one gulp.

When they got back to the cabin, everyone crowded around after one look at Earl's pale, drained face.

"I'll tell you one thing," he said. "If it wasn't for this man right here, you boys wouldn't be bothered with ole Earl any more. That damn shark was all over me after those fish, and how he missed my legs I'll never know. When he hit, I'd just felt the stringer come by me in a wave and had kicked it out of the way. That damn quick-release stringer works just fine when there ain't no pressure on it, but when that shark grabbed them fish and yanked me down, that thing held like it was tied to me! And then here comes ole Neal, cool as a cucumber, yellin' at that shark like a cowboy in a herd of goats, and reaches right down in the middle of 'em and gets me loose."

About that time Neal looked down at his wrist watch, and he felt a big knot come up in his stomach. He took a long drink from the glass.

"Dammit, I got to go," he said. "I'm supposed to be back in Houston by seven-thirty."

Frankie Edwards, who had been drinking beer all day around the cabin, cackled out loud.

"Now if that ain't something! Man's a hero with a herd of sharks but scared of his old lady."

Neal took another drink.

"A man ain't scared of anything that ain't scared of a ten-foot shark," Earl said. "He's just tryin' to avoid unpleasantness."

Felix asked if Neal couldn't at least stay long enough to have a bite of gumbo, and besides they needed a guitar player because Rusty was coming over to play the piano after a while and probably Hal would be down, and no telling who else.

"You couldn't just claim to have car trouble or something?" Earl suggested. "We'd all back you up on it. And to tell the truth," he added significantly, "it might do you good, old man. You ain't been looking your best lately, and I noticed even before we got into them sharks you was shaking pretty good even tryin' to pour a drink. Man's nerves have to be considered same as his obligations."

Neal thought about it, and he knew they were right. He took another drink of bourbon.

"Tell you what, I'll drive up the road and call her. Maybe we can get out of that deal tonight."

The beer joint down the road was loud and crowded, and he closed the phone booth door and put one finger in his ear to hear better. For the first time in a month, his hands were not shaking when he dialed the number.

"Where in the world are you, Neal? You sound as if you're at a party or something. You're not still in Galveston?"

"Helen, baby, is there any possible way we can get out of meeting the Winstons tonight? I mean I'm really enjoying being with the guys again, sort of relaxing for a change. You know what's been going on at the office and all. Couldn't you just tell 'em I had car trouble or something and that we can get together with them any night next week?"

"Of course, dear, if that's what you want. You know, of course, it was I who invited them, and I rather expect they would have made other plans for a Saturday night had they not been committed to be with us."

"Now Helen, Harry Winston doesn't have a thing to do all week, Saturdays or otherwise, that he doesn't want to do. He inherited his, and I'm still trying to make ours. Now I've about had it; I've been nervous lately, my work hasn't been good, and I feel this is important for both of us if I just loosen up a little this weekend."

He could hear her beginning to sniffle, and he knew she

would be crying big, silent tears behind the glasses. He had never been able to decide if Helen could cry when she wanted to, or if it just worked out that way.

"Forget it," he said, "I'm heading in. There won't be time to eat, just put out my gray suit and call the Winstons and tell them we'll be a few minutes late."

"Oh, no, dear," she sniffled. "I really don't mind. I'm just being silly. You do need to get away. I'll make out just fine and I'll see you Sunday night."

"You really don't mind?"

"No," she sobbed. "You catch plenty of fish."

He heard the receiver click in his ear and then the empty dial tone. A teen-ager was waiting for the phone, and he got up wearily and walked out into the soft, humid air which was already cooling for the sunset.

A couple of white gulls hovered overhead in the breeze, sailing wild and free, and he sat down in the car and poured a heavy slug of bourbon from the plastic flask.

Maybe he was being selfish. Hal would probably be down a couple of days and maybe it would be possible to get back one day in the week and see him. And Harry Winston was the sort of investor who could do a man some good.

He took a sip of the bourbon, noticed his fingers were shaking again, but the safety belt snapped into place from habit. If he took the back road, he could be home by eight, and Harry Winston was always a little late anyway.

Behind the cabin in West Bay, Earl and Frankie had waded out the mouth of the old slough behind the fence, caught a half-dozen small trout, and were cleaning them and waiting on Neal to fillet his surf string.

A car horn honked far across the island on the main road, and they saw Neal's Cadillac hitting ninety into the sunset.

"Goddam shame, ain't it," Earl said. "Left his tackle and hat and the whole works, and I expect he'll catch hell about that, too, when he gets home."

"Yeah," said Frankie, "which is one good thing about sharks. When they start eatin' on a man at least he knows it. But that woman will kill him just as sure as my old lady would've killed me a-workin' if I'd let her."

From across the island the old piano began plinking, and they gutted and gilled Neal's string of trout in a hurry because Rusty was already there.

"Good ole Rusty," Frankie chuckled. "Never gave a woman the time of day in his life, an' they all love him for it."

"Uh huh," mused Earl. "And if Neal ever found out about him and Helen, I reckon it would just about kill ole Neal, now wouldn't it?"

Anatomy of a Goose Hunt

As with most invasions, it begins with breakfast in the middle of the night, when no one wants any. Little rice-country cafés swarm with strange faces at 4:00 a.m. board floors vibrate with clumping boots, goose callers, juke boxes, laughter and back-slapping greetings between old friends who have come from far places. Sleepy-eyed tycoons in tunics from Abercrombie's and Neiman's pull up extra chairs to rub elbows with tenant farmers in staples from Sears . . . because the farmers live here, and there is no status quite like that of a goose guide on opening day.

Provisioned with tactical information, pockets filled with spare Rolaids, flashlights, cigarettes, handwarmers, candy bars, and aspirin . . . the first waves hurriedly pull on white coveralls and ski parkas outside the cafés, using the light to dress because it will be inky dark in the ricefields.

The white clothing is designed to blend their bulkiness into decoy spreads of white rags or papers which, in turn, are supposed to resemble great concentrations of geese. Instead, the audiovisual impression is of a hurriedly called meeting of the Ku Klux Klan.

Along the back roads of the flat coastal plain, dusty fingers of car lights probe the darkness. There is a muffled shuffling in the dark, a match flickers and an ember glows and bobs in the darkness, a cigarette cough racks unpolluted country air.

An old snow goose, his black wing tips the chevrons of age and authority, raises his head in alarm. He has been in this kind of trouble before. To him, it is D-Day.

Already in the dark sky above he can hear other geese, from other roosts, in flight long before their normal dawn departure. They have been frightened by the probing lights and by hunters moving into blinds on their roosting ponds, and the wind brings their warning clearly to the old snow.

The bulky figures stumbling through the stubble can also hear the distant clamor, a yelling, shrieking cacophony rising and falling with the wind as if somewhere high in the sky Comanches are circling a wagon train.

In the rush to get out decoys, there is no caste system. Millionaires grunt, groan, and flutter out white rags upon the stubble alongside schoolboys and service station attendants . . . all having been created equal in the eyes of the landowner who accepted their fifteen dollars apiece.

Huddled behind a levee, a Chinese cashier and a Mexican waiter from the same restaurant are creating a din comparable to that emanating from the goose roost.

"You didn't bling no gun?"

"*Si,* a thirty-two."

"Model 32 Klieghoff or Lemington?"

"*Quien sabe?*" the Mexican pulled the pistol and pointed it at the sky. "All I know, my brother says is .32."

"Nobody shoot goose with pistol, goddammit."

"Why? In the movies they shoot Indians off horses with pistols and Indians are tougher than geese, *amigo.*"

Across the levee in the cold mud of the ricefield, a Houston banker hollows out a spot for hips and elbows, bones and joints creaking. He carefully spreads out a white rag beside him and puts out extra shells where he can get to them in a hurry.

The sky lightens in the east, and suddenly the old snow goose compresses his feathers, hauls back his head, and shrieks a shrill, piercing cry of warning. In a mighty thunder of wings, five thousand snows, blues and Canadas rend the skies, a dark funnel cloud above the pink horizon.

As if by the signal, the air is filled with strange whistlings of wings, quacks, yelps, and squeaks from other ricefield residents fortunate enough not to be geese . . . cranes, herons, ibis, bitterns, and the sudden, high-frequency swoosh, nature's nearest to the sonic boom, a flight of teal dodging four feet over the stubble and out of sight in an instant like fighter planes over the skirmish lines.

The geese, being led higher and higher by the old black-tipped snow, have survived man's tribes for centuries, evolving intelligence to cope with marsh fires, punt guns, and now the Power-Piston, Mark 5 and magnum. They have prospered, taking advantage of this most recent civilization's bounty of rice, stealing it from the fields within sight of the villages.

By heredity the U-2 of waterfowl, the old snow knows he can live by gaining altitude, and that is what he is doing as the first salvos of a new season *carrrrump* across the prairies and ricefields.

The young of the year struggling to climb behind him started their transcontinental migration from the Arctic with fledgling feathers and intelligence, following their parents by instinct. But the old snow knows that when they become tired and hungry they will begin to take interest in the great white patches on the ground below which look so much like other geese, but which can suddenly bristle black sticks that shoot fire and death into the sky.

The old snow warns them with a low, guttural grunting and they climb higher.

The banker's guide below is a rice farmer who has carefully judged the first flights by a strip of timber on the horizon. The old snow has led them too high for any shotgun. But behind them a smaller gaggle of confused young birds is leaving the roosting pond, and instinctively the guide knows they are coming.

"When I start calling, don't move a muscle," he commands. "And nobody shoots or moves until I call the shot."

The young geese have seen the white on the ground, and they have ignored the screaming, yelling warnings of the old snow up front. They are hungry, and they cup wings to look. Two young blues are convinced and begin their greeting clamor, and the whole flight begins sideslipping and whiffling down like falling white leaves toward the decoys.

The guide is stumbling to his feet.

"All right, let's get 'em!"

Guns blast streaks of fire into the sky and heavy, rice-fed bodies whop into muddy soil. The old snow looks down sorrowfully and climbs higher. In his war, as with all others, it is the young who go first.

The sun rises and warms the stubble, and black rice-birds flutter among white rags of decoys. Yellow-breasted meadowlarks perch on bloodweed stalks along the canals and sing their invariable greeting to the morning, oblivious of the guns going off around them.

The old warden sitting in the back of a pickup truck on the highest knoll in the countryside sees the show for miles around through powerful binoculars and a tripod-mounted spotting scope.

He shakes his head as a flight of six whitefronts cup wings and head into a spread of white rags in which six hunters are sitting upright, towering over their rag decoys more like a village of Indian tepees on the prairie.

The warden cannot understand how the smartest of waterfowl can do this foolish thing. But he has seen them do it from James Bay in the far north, where the Cree Indians use goose wings on sticks, to the Louisiana marshes, where twisted newspapers spread upon the marsh grass trick them into range.

He knows the goose's weakness is numbers, because his ancestral safety has been in numbers. It is difficult for man or animal to stalk a great concentration of feeding snows and blues on the ground, because there are a thousand sentinels watching at once. Thus, the larger the concentration the safer it seems to a goose, and the larger the spread of white rags on the ground the more likely it is to lull the young birds into false security.

The warden wonders if someday man will find the perfect decoy, or the ultimate shotgun, but then he smiles to himself and cocks an ear to the rising north wind.

From overhead, somewhere high in the blue brilliance of sun and sky, comes the derisive, high-pitched cry of the old black-tipped snow . . . far out of range of the Mark V or the magnum, the Chinaman and the banker, or perhaps even from the law of the land, and the warden enforcing it.

The old snow has survived his longest morning of the year . . . as he will survive a winter of shot and shell . . . streamlined proof of a protection older than the concrete pueblo or the Power-Piston.

As long as his homeland is spared by the plow, and the stars are there to guide him south upon the north winds each fall, he can stand off man's civilization for centuries to come, a noble snow-white symbol of the wild whose cries in the night sky will cause dogs to howl and men to sit up in bed stirred by the same primitive instincts of the hunter.

And back in the little rice-country café, a weary waitress in coffee-stained uniform sinks to a counter stool, lights a cigarette, and wonders what in the world a grown man wants with a goose.

The Naming of Rattlesnake Road

Sam Gorman knew there was trouble when he turned off the gravel road into the lease. The fence gap was down, pulled off to one side and just left there. And in the thirty years he and his father before him had been on the lease, that gap had never been left down.

He stopped and closed it, gunned the station wagon with the cut-down Volkswagen dune buggy in tow, and drove straight up to the cabin. Sure enough, there was a strange car there, a new

Lincoln, and the Mexican caretaker was sitting on the front porch as if in a mild state of shock.

"What's going on, José?"

"No se'. Thees man come, say he buy out Meester Smeeth. He gone hunt already. Plenty trouble, maybe. He shoot right here in ground." José made the motion of letting a gun go off.

Sam unloaded the station wagon and pondered the problem. There were six of them in on the lease, some of the best quail country between Cuero and Goliad. It had been a family thing, with memberships handed down from father to son for years. He couldn't understand how anybody could buy out Lonnie Smith.

Buzz Graham came driving up from Cuero with the dog wagon behind the Jeep, and Sam piled in with him and began telling him the problem.

Buzz had already heard. Smith was in some kind of financial strait and had to sell half interest in his business. He'd been carrying the hunting lease as a business expense all those years, and the new partner had demanded use of the facilities. Lonnie was so shaken up about it he hadn't sobered up in a week.

Suddenly a shotgun blast at close range rent the air. Buzz slammed on the brakes and a crippled quail with one leg hanging almost flew into the windshield.

The man who stepped out from the prickly pear bush was bespectacled and quite small, incongruous in cowboy boots and white porkpie hat, and there was a distinct scowl on his pinkish face.

"I've been stalking that covey for half a mile," he said stiffly, "and I was just getting ready to shoot when you gentlemen chose to drive right into them."

Buzz looked back at him with remarkable control. "Do you realize," he said, "that the covey you were stalking, as you put it, happens to be the house covey which has been fed out the back door of that cabin for more than twenty years? And do you realize, sir, it is not considered particularly sporting to either stalk or shoot into a covey of bobwhite quail on the ground?"

The little man shoved the clean, white porkpie hat back on

his head, and said coolly that he was now one of the owners of the lease, and that he would shoot his quail when and where he chose.

It was then that Buzz noticed the delicate lines of the little 20-gauge Parker double; there was no mistaking it, the pride and joy of Robbie Adams, beautiful muzzles now resting in the dirt as the little man leaned on the stock.

"Did you buy that gun, too?" Buzz sputtered, choking back the rage.

"No, it was up in the cabin. I just borrowed it."

Sam stepped forward, thought better of it, and stuck out his hand and introduced them both. "If you don't mind, I'll let you shoot my old pumpgun here," he said, picking up the 28-gauge out of the Jeep. "I'm afraid Robbie might get a little unhappy; you see, that gun has been in his family for three generations and it's sort of more than a gun to him."

"Fine," said the little man, taking the 28-gauge. "How do you load this one?"

They left him walking the fencerow, with the excuse that they had to check out the country for the next morning's hunt.

"What are we gonna do?" Sam groaned. "You realize what would have happened if Robbie had come up on that little jerk instead of us?"

"I wish he had," said Buzz.

"No, there's some other way to do it without a killing."

They saw plenty of quail, one big covey ran across the road in front of them, but neither was in the mood to hunt. Then Sam saw a big diamondback rattler slither out of the ruts into a pear bush. He backed up and killed it with his .22 pistol.

"Did you see that little guy jump when I cautioned him to watch for snakes on that fencerow?" he said thoughtfully.

"Yeah, but we're not that lucky; he could probably crawl through a pear bush and not get bit."

"Doesn't have to get bit if he gets scared enough," Sam said, getting out to pick up the snake. "We'll just show up with this baby in the back of the Jeep and he'll at least start thinking about snakes."

At the cabin that night, José served a real Mexican *comida*—
chunks of venison in ranch beans, flavored with chili powder and
with some fresh *jalapeños* and soft tortillas on the side.

"These quail are tricky little rascals, aren't they?" the little
man was saying, pulling off the incongruously tiny cowboy boots.
"Even if you shoot one, you have to watch that he's stone dead or
he'll get away. One ran into a hole under a prickly pear on me
today, and I had to reach in there all the way up to my elbow to
get him."

"You did what?" Buzz choked on a *jalapeño*. "Man, do you
know you're lucky to be alive right now?"

"Why?"

"Because that hole you ran your hand into very likely had
from one to three rattlesnakes in it!"

"Now look, boys, let's don't sell each other short," the little
man smiled, pitching the cowboy boots in the general direction of
the sleeping porch. "I didn't expect to be welcomed on this lease
with open arms, but don't insult my intelligence by telling me
there are three rattlesnakes in every hole on this ranch."

Sam excused himself, and Buzz shook his head and picked
up a magazine, wondering if Sam was going to bring in the big
rattlesnake now or wait until morning.

Instead, Sam came back off the porch, where the bunks
were, with a concerned look on his face.

"You say you didn't even see a single snake today?" he
asked the little man.

"Not a sign of one."

"Well, one saw you."

"How do you mean?"

Sam held one of the tiny cowboy boots under the light, and
hanging from the back side were the broken fangs of a very large
rattlesnake.

"You didn't feel something sort of peck your leg when you
were walking through the cactus today?" Sam asked innocently.
"You're lucky, because a snake this size could have hit you at the
knees as easily as the ankles."

The little man paled, recovered his composure, and told the

Mexican to pull the fangs out of his boot. The Mexican would not touch them. Sam put on heavy gloves and made a very big project out of extracting them, explaining that one drop of the venom could kill a man more or less instantly.

They turned in early, and all night long the little man dreamed he heard rattlesnakes rattling. Which he had, because Sam had tied the rattles from the dead snake on a string just outside his window where the wind could shake them.

The next morning, Sam gave José a ride to the north fence-line to burn some prickly pear for the rancher, not really feeling like hunting anyway, and helped the Mexican carry the blowtorch, wondering how the devil a cow ever ate cactus with the spines burned off . . . and also how civilized men could go about getting rid of a pest more serious than stickers.

The little man had insisted he hunt with them that afternoon, because they had the dogs, and Sam drove the dune buggy like a madman through the brush, scaring only himself and Buzz.

Periodically they stopped to search for coveys under the cactus with binoculars, hoping to see snakes but finding instead the most quail they'd had on the lease in five years. The little man killed his first two birds on the wing and also learned to keep the safety on the 28-gauge until the dogs pointed, a practice initiated by Buzz after it was learned he'd been carrying the loaded gun for two days cocked and ready to fire.

"Beautiful!" said Buzz when they got away from him after dinner. "We hunt all day and see one lousy rattlesnake, the little bastard hits his first quail, and now he's just likely to move down here and camp for the rest of the season."

"I doubt it," smiled Sam mischievously. "I've got to go talk to José."

They were sipping a brandy when the Mexican came up about bedtime with a worried look.

"Turn cold tonight," he said. "Don' nobody goes outside."

"What's he mean by that?" the little man asked.

"Oh, a little problem we have down here sometimes with the first few northers," Sam yawned. "This country's full of snakes, like we told you, and sometimes when it starts gettin'

cold they come out of those holes and migrate, regular swarms of
'em."

"Where do they go?"

"Aw, they're tryin' to find a warm place, and that's what
the Mexican's talking about. Sometimes they'll try to get into the
house or the barn. One year up here we killed over two hundred
snakes right here in the yard, and half the guys on the lease got
bitten before it was over."

"Yeah," said Buzz, "and does it smart when somebody has
to cut that big x-mark on the bite. Sam nearly butchered my leg
off that year, see the scar?"

The little man sat up in bed and Buzz flicked the flashlight
on an ugly, gaping scar on the calf of his leg which had been put
there by a rock from a lawnmower.

"Why do you have to make a cut like that?"

"To suck out the poison."

"Yeah," said Sam. "Get hit on the pecker, and that's when you really find out who your friends are."

The next morning dawned clear and cold, and they started hunting from the house, because Sam said there were three big coveys that roosted in the open field just behind it, and he wanted to get into them before they got back into the snake brush.

They were walking up a little trail when one of the dogs suddenly came down on a half-point, wagged his tail, whined, and Sam shot right under his nose. A huge diamondback rattler rolled over belly up.

About that time, José yelled, firing his .22 pistol to the left into the brush, and Sam began blazing away to the right.

"They're all around us!" he yelled to Buzz. "Let's kill as many as we can and back out of here. It looks like the migration!"

The little man was peering into the brush, and now he could see them, coiled and ready to strike; they were everywhere; he shot three and saw them flop over. He was loading and shooting as fast as he could, backing up, and he almost tripped over one in the trail.

Suddenly the sheer terror of them gripped him, he backed faster, then turned and ran, throwing down the 28-gauge, grabbing for his glasses, running for all the tiny cowboy boots coulc' do.

José was sitting down on the ground, laughing so hard he could not get up again, and Sam was slapping him on the back, tears of mirth streaming down his face. Buzz was not exactly sure what was going on, except that he heard the Lincoln fire up back at the cabin, and the brush scratching the sides of the car as it flew past on the road.

Then he realized that not one of those fifteen or so snakes shot had ever moved a muscle.

"Where," he said, starting to laugh incredulously, "did you fools get all those dead rattlesnakes?"

"Me gotte," whooped José, eyes bleary from the laughing. "Me gotte all day; burn pear, shoot rattlesnake, burn more pear. Puttee fire in hole, plenty snake come out, plenty .22 shell, whole box all shooted."

"I guess we better get going before every cow in the pasture gets out," Sam said, holding his side and helping José up. "I expect there's a gap or two down someplace . . . up there on Rattlesnake Road."

The Cry of the Hen

Little Duck leaned forward and skylighted the top of the cane, searching for the faint glimmer of starlight on water which would be the winding boat road leading to No. 15 blind.

"Hot damn!" he cursed under his breath, as a stalk of dew-wet cane almost swiped the figure huddled in the bow. If there were two things about guiding he hated it would be taking out a woman and trying to work mallards in an east wind!

"Why do they call you Little Duck?" the woman was asking, tongue a little thick from the party that had gone on all night long in the big guest house at the hunting club.

"Wellum, pappa was Big Duck Broussard, and everybody knowed him by that name, so I guess me, I got to be Little Duck."

"What is your real name?"

"Emile."

"Why, that's a beautiful name, and that's what I'm going to call you, Emile."

"Yessum."

He shoved the push pole harder; it would be almost shooting time when he got out the decoys.

"How old are you, Emile?"

"Sixteen."

"You're such a big, strong boy; do you play football at school?"

"No'm, when Big Duck's shrimp boat blowed up on him, it left us with no pappa and no boat, and me I got three brothers and a sister, wasn't no time for school."

"How terrible! Didn't your father have insurance?"

"Yessum, but not enough."

A bunch of mallards thundered up in the darkness ahead and he knew they were nearing the blind, because that was where the mallards would have been sitting. He had cut that opening in the cane himself.

"What is that sound, Emile?"

"A mallard hen."

"Now how can you possibly know if that duck was a mallard, and even if you did, whether it was a drake or a hen?"

"Wellum, there ain't no other duck calls exactly like a mallard, and it's the hen that does all the calling."

"In other words, just as with people, the women do all the talking," she laughed musically. "Isn't that right, Emile?"

"Yessum, I mean, no'm."

"You're trying to be so polite, Emile, and really I'd like for you to think of me as a friend, not just some stuffy old lady married to one of the big shots that belong to the club."

"Yessum, I guess we're just about there. If you'd sit steady until I get up in the blind, then I can hold the boat for you while you get out."

He got into the blind first with the flashlight, kicked some nutria droppings off the seat and wiped it off with the sleeve of his jacket. Then he helped her out of the boat and pulled it behind the blind and made sure the brush covered it perfectly.

"Would you like a cigarette, Emile?"

"No'm."

"You know my husband, don't you, Emile?"

"Yessum."

"You don't have to call me 'yessum'; my name is Evelyn or if you prefer, Mrs. Bordeaux. You're just as white as I am, and I told you we're just hunting buddies, didn't I?"

He started to say yessum, panicked because he couldn't

think of anything else, and reached for the little cane-bodied caller around his neck and blew a couple of loud highballs into it, limbering up the reed and feeling his face reddening because he didn't know what to say.

She reached beneath the bench and came up with the thermos jug he had so carefully hidden under there so that it wouldn't shine and scare the ducks.

"Would you like a Bloody Mary, Emile?"

"No'm."

"Now what did I tell you to call me?"

"You said not to call you 'yessum,'" he smiled, and suddenly she realized how cleancut and handsome he was in the early light, purely and simply French, not Cajun, the Gallic nose, smooth skin, rosy cheeks of the Acadians who settled the Evangeline country.

"Right over there about two hundred yards, in that next bunch of tall cane, is where Mr. Bordeaux and my little brother is huntin'," he told her. "My brother, he's a good duck caller. You hear him?"

They were sitting side by side, head and shoulders above the brush of the blind, and he showed her how to lean slightly forward into the brush of the blind to hide without sitting down, and still be able to see. Suddenly, somewhere across the marsh, a shotgun boomed and reverberated in the timber, and teal, gadwalls, widgeon, black mallards, spoonbills, herons, egrets and roosting rice birds from the edge of the marsh swarmed into the air, wave after wave of different bodies designed for different speeds, crossing the orange sky.

He could sense her excitement. "Don't move," he whispered. "I'll say when, and you take the ones on the right; pick out the greenheads."

A flight of northern mallards were cupping wings, losing altitude, looking for the protection of the tall cane. Emile blew hard and high, making the caller break over into a high-pitched squeal, as a hen sometimes cracks her voice in excitement.

The lead drake cupped wings, almost halted in midair, listening. And from the sky behind him came back the same high, three-note, downpitching cry of excited greeting he had made with the caller. He'd convinced one hen anyway.

They were back-pedaling out of the clouds, white breasts of the drakes glowing orange in the sunrise, making all the squeaks, squawks, and tiny sounds no man can make, a majestic drake in the lead, eyes focused on the decoys.

"Now," said Emile softly, and he waited until the first crack of the little 20-gauge before he pulled two feet ahead of the drake at the rear, saw him shudder and fold; then found another drake straining upward, wings beating for altitude as he collapsed into a shower of white feathers. Emile waited for the second bark of the 20-gauge, but it never came.

She was looking up strangely at him, eyes shining, gun smoking.

"Emile, it was magnificent! I knew I would miss, and I did, but I watched you and you were simply perfection; you could have killed three but you waited for me."

"Why didn't you shoot the second barrel?" he asked.

"Because I was watching you."

The way she looked at him suddenly embarrassed him. Two widgeon hovered over high and she watched him call, pleading into the little cane cylinder with the reed he had painstakingly whittled from a rubber comb, the vein in his neck pulsing, and the rosy Acadian cheeks blushed with the vibrant blood of the young.

"You have such big legs, Emile. Do you lift weights or something?"

"No'm," he breathed, slightly out of breath from the calling. "This marsh makes big legs if you walk it much. Either that or you don't walk it much."

It seemed perfectly natural that she should touch his leg, and he tightened the muscle, as instinctively as a male dog stiffens his hackles.

Then suddenly he was embarrassed.

"Maybe I could take just one little taste of that tomato juice," he said, as if someone else were saying it.

The Bloody Mary was strong, with Louisiana pepper and

vodka, and the perfumed smell of her hand was on the cup. He drank it in two deep drafts, as his pappa had taught him to drink, like a man.

High V's of geese, snow-white against the blue sky, were leaving the marsh for the rice fields, mostly snows and blues, with a few brown specklebellies and Canadas.

She thrilled to the spectacle, and to the vodka, and he showed her the black wing tips of the mature snows, which he called brant, the drab whiteness of the young of the year, and the pure-white heads and bluish bodies of the old blues.

"If you listen," he said, "you can tell the difference in the brant. The high, clear voices are the old ones; the coarse, raspy ones are the young."

"Do only their hens call?"

He shook his head. "They're Cajun brant," he smiled, feeling the vodka, "they all talk all the time." She poured another red plastic cup from the thermos, brimming to the top.

Even in the big four-man blind, they were sitting close together and he felt her hand again on his leg.

The sun was bright and he could not stand to look at her. He looked across the marsh, at the things he knew, and felt the hand move up, and up, until there was no longer any doubt of destination.

"I don't see," she murmured softly, "how they ever called you Little Duck."

He watched the marsh, feeling his face flush, stronger motivations moving him as powerfully and naturally as the vodka and the pulsing vein in his neck.

He heard her clothing, the zippers, and the smell of perfume wafted up from inside the down jacket which was now on the long, wooden bench of the blind and he was seeing without looking, watching the other blind less than two hundred yards away.

"We could hear their motor in plenty of time," she was saying casually. "I know what you must think of me, but please don't think just now, Emile. Someday you will understand, when you are older and you see a girl of sixteen. You will need something to remember, someone to think of when you are making love to someone you may not really love . . . and you will understand me then, Emile."

Her hands were moving, and they knew where, and how, and in no man, of sixteen or sixty, is their restraint beyond reason.

He turned and saw her, in the full light of the sun, unashamed and alabaster, white smoothness of skin, blond bushiness of the Nordic races he had never seen, and a sudden compelling force in that instant reduced the world to one capsule of sky and cane and warmth and euphoria, and it was over almost before it began.

Somewhere in the distance, beyond the sensations and softness, came the haunting, mocking cry which moved him instinctively to look up. The mallards were hanging low over the blind, orange feet starting down . . . watched by the husband across the marsh and by Emile's brother . . . and if they were not shot there would be explaining to do. Emile was in no position to shoot.

In that instant, the great protector of young dogs, and young men, perhaps Satan himself, told him what to do and Emile blew his caller as loud as ever in his life, the harsh strident alarm call of the wild mallard.

The ducks fell back with the wind, instantly out of range.

That night at the big lodge, Emile was invited (as guides so rarely are) to have dinner with the guests of the big house, and he wore his best shirt, open at the neck because he owned only one tie for funerals, and his best shoes and pants, which were both black.

"Damn shame what Evelyn did to you today, old boy," Mr. Bordeaux said as he passed the crawfish *étouffé*. "I knew she couldn't be still in a duck blind, and when that bunch of mallards dropped in right on top of you I knew what had happened before she ever told me . . . she just had to move and spook 'em."

Emile felt the blood in his cheeks and the light kick against his calf under the table.

"I had them coming in," he blurted, "but I guess I held a quack a little too long, and they thought it was the alarm call. It really wasn't her fault at all."

"Little Duck, you are a real gentleman," Evelyn said lightly, spearing a crawfish. "It's a shame we can't stay over one more day and give you and me a chance to redeem ourselves."

Everybody laughed, except Little Duck inside.

And that night as the big Cajun moon rose over the cypress along the bayou, he turned and tossed and rumpled the sheets in the desire and torment of the young, and heard on the rising wind the haunting call he for the first time fully understood . . . the lonely, lovely, lustful cry of the hen.

The Holly Beach Hurricane

Luther Mallory went barefoot most of the time in a dirty under-shirt and baggy khakis, undisputed king of camp, surveying his domain from a big wooden rocking chair of a throne high on the covered porch overlooking the canal at Port Isabel.

This particular morning, when the first sleepy-eyed fish-ermen began arriving, he just kept sitting.

"I'm selling no bait today," he announced. "If you want to go out and kill yourselves, buy it across the street."

Charlie Babcock, who had silver hair and fifteen years as a paying customer, went on loading his boat.

"Kill ourselves? How?"

Luther snorted. "You can't read the signs? You can't see there's a storm coming?"

"Radio didn't say anything about a storm."

"Fine, then you go by the radio."

The others gathered, respecting Charlie, vaguely fearing Luther.

"OK," said Charlie, "so the barometer's falling fast. I've noticed that too. But this is Valentine's Day, old buddy. We don't get real storms in February, just bad northers."

Luther rocked in his chair, smoking his pipe, watching his pet squirrels tearing up their treadmill and the big green Mexican jungle parrot walking nervously up and down his cage, squawking the one word he had picked up from Luther, which was "sonofabitch."

"For your edification," Luther said, allowing the big word to sink in, "I am hereby predicting a hurricane to hit here by late this afternoon. And if I might make one suggestion, it would be to fish on this side of the lagoon because there should be some redfish down around Holly Beach on the storm tide ahead of this thing, and also because some of you just might be able to get to high ground where I can pick you up, provided I get everything done around here."

There was a chorus of hooraws and yelps, and outboards began firing up, wet and balky from the humidity.

"That's what happens when a man quits drinkin' in his old age," Charlie yelled above the sputtering of his old Johnson. "Quit lubricatin' an old mind and it's liable to rust and lock up on somethin' like a February hurricane!"

He idled along the channel, respecting the four-mile speed limit past the yacht marina, and then cruised out into the Laguna past the channel marker where the trout and skipjack school under the gulls every summer. To the right, Queen Isabella Causeway was almost obscured by a hazy sort of fog, and the Padre Island shoreline was a mirage with the tops of the dunes showing above the water.

Jack Curren, several years younger, kept looking at the sky as he rigged his tackle. "Sky sure does look funny, doesn't it? You get to thinking about it, we haven't had any real winter this year, and the temperature is about the same as it is in fall hurricane season."

"Aw, come on," Charlie groaned. "There's not a hurricane in history this time of year. Only thing bothering me is the barometer; I've seen the trout really take lockjaw with the glass falling this fast."

He cruised to the west of the Intracoastal, feeling the rising waves help the old Ashburn hull along, and knowing he would take a terrible butt-beating on the way back.

Luther had been right about one thing; the tide was well above the usual mark on the trotline stakes they passed, and probably still rising. The redfish might indeed be tearing it up at Holly Beach.

He turned out of the channel over to the south shore, and watched for fish slicks in the shallow water.

The King Ranch shoreline was strangely dead, no deer nor turkey, not even a coyote. And when he dropped over the drag anchor, there was some four feet of water where there should have been three.

The boat swung around to the anchor, and he shot the gold spoon high where the wind would carry it. As he took up slack on the great wind-belly in the line, the spoon skittered across the surface and the surface exploded, jolting his long popping rod into a throbbing curve.

"Throw in beside me," he yelled. "There may be a school!"

Jack flipped a short cast behind the hooked fish, cranked three times fast to keep the spoon out of the grass, and his own rod doubled.

Not far across the bay, other boats were watching the action through binoculars. Motors cranked, and the race was on. Charlie pointed toward the fish and waved for them to go upwind and drift rather than crossing the school.

"Ease out the big anchor," he yelled above the rising wind. "Let's hold right here."

Jack fought the bucking rod with one hand and the anchor

line with the other, and eased the Danforth down to the spongy bottom, feeling it catch and slip twice, then grab solidly as the boat swerved into the wind.

The wind blew Charlie's next cast into a floating mass of eel grass. He reeled in furiously to clean off the spoon, and had a tremendous surface strike as a seven-pound red streaked off across the flats. Out of the corner of his eye he saw the next boat with both rods bending, drifting straight toward a row of trotline stakes. He tried to yell into the wind to warn them, but it was too late; the boat hit the almost invisible monofilament line with its deadly row of hooks dangling at the surface. Both men flattened into the boat, and one held up the line and pulled them safely under. Charlie saw a knifeblade flash as the man in the bow cut the line. Good! He too hated those trotlines with a vengeance.

As he fought the red, he wondered how the fish had survived to be this size with the thousands of trotline hooks, the illegal netters operating with airboats and airplanes, the "pot-lickers" who'll keep any baby red they can catch, even though the Laguna Madre was the first saltwater in Texas to have a minimum size limit set by law.

The trotlines, he figured, were the worst of all.

Baited with only strips of thin plastic, they are set at the surface so that at night, when the Laguna winds blow, the plastic flaps and wriggles at the surface. Redfish, particularly, seem susceptible to strips, mistaking them perhaps for baitfish, and Charlie had seen lines filled with bloated, crab-eaten reds because some commercial fisherman stayed drunk too long in Isabel or Matamoros.

In the old days, it had not been so bad. The lines were made of cotton, and couldn't be left out all the time, and natural bait was used on the hooks, so that the lines had to be run often. Even the large posts holding up the lines, and the "gates" signifying safe passageways through the hooks, were once kept well marked with burlap sacks or bright cloth. Now they were often left unattended for months, hazards to man and fish alike.

The tide was still rising, flooding the shallow flats along the shoreline, and the water was alive with fish. A porpoise rolled beside the boat, exhaled with an audible snort, and Charlie threw his reel into free spool to let the redfish run; sometimes porpoises are as bad as sharks about hitting a hooked fish. Far back against the shoreline, a school of reds, or maybe big jackfish, exploded into a series of blasts and swirls, and mullet arced into the air like silver missiles, racing for the shallow water which is their only sanctuary.

A school of tarpon swept past the boat, moving fast and purposefully, brownish backs out of water as they crossed the shallow ledge, not rolling but hunting, moving into the rising flood of the tide in the shallows.

The boat was bobbing and pitching like a cork in white-capping waves, and the sun had become an obscure orb in a strange, metallic-bronze sky. Far across the Laguna, a sheet of rain was advancing from Padre Island.

"Let's get the hell outa here," Jack yelled. "I'm coming up with the anchor."

The boat was racing with the wind for the shoreline and shallower water when the cold rain pelted them with stinging force. It closed in around them, the ominous, cold breath of the storm, howling, pelting, wailing wind and rain surrounding them, blinding them, the surface hissing with the impact of the sheets and blasts of rain.

"I'm gonna run for the shoreline, straight in as far as we can get," Charlie yelled. "When she stops, jump out and we'll pull her far as we can and then turn around to face it."

They roared in until the prop began bumping bottom, and as Jack jumped, whitecaps came pouring in over the transom. They shoved her bow into the gale, put out both anchors, stumbling and falling in the mucky bottom, and started for shore.

Jack held his hand, and the two of them fought it together for the last hundred yards, falling and crawling, hoping they were going in the right direction. Only by feel, the gradual hardening of bottom and the larger, harder clumps of grass, could they find the mainland. The wind was now a brutal force, shoving them bodily with its gusts, sucking the breath from their mouths, and they panted and half ran, half stumbled in the stinging, blinding rain. Somewhere, not far, Charlie knew there was a fence. There would be driftwood piled along the fence and they could lie down behind it for some sort of shelter. Surely this thing, whatever it was, couldn't last long.

Four miserable, freezing hours later, the wind began to ease. They had been pelted with flying driftwood; lying flat behind the fence, backs to the gale, and in all his life on the coast, Charlie had never heard a wind howl and scream with such vengeance.

Far off in the darkness they could see two tiny beams of headlights. They stumbled for them, yelling for the others, getting no answer. Charlie was shivering uncontrollably.

The lights seemed to grow nearer, then farther, obscured by the gusts of rain. Then finally they were close enough to hear a hoarse profanity, which, at the moment, was sweeter than the singing of angels.

"Hurry up," Luther was yelling, yellow slicker flapping in the car lights. "No tellin' where them other dumb sonofabitches are."

The next morning dawned ominously still. Wreckage of bait boxes, boats, and debris floated in the little channel below where Luther sat in the wooden rocking chair. The bruised and bleary-eyed assemblage around him stood transfixed, listening to the little black transistor radio.

"The U.S. Weather Bureau at New Orleans has just issued the following announcement. Pictures transmitted from the U.S. weather satellite indicate a vague circular cloud pattern and the disturbance is now moving up the Louisiana coast. Heavy damage to fishing camps, vessels at sea, and the citrus crops of the Rio Grande Valley has been reported, with tides running up to eight feet above normal."

Luther reached over and shut off the radio and leaned back in the big rocking chair.

"They're not going to call it a hurricane when they didn't give a word of warning ahead of it," he grumbled. "Now I guess we'll have to fight the insurance companies all over again on whether we even had a storm."

"All I want to know," said Charlie Babcock, "is how you knew about it."

"Smart sonofabitch," croaked the parrot. And it was the only time any of them ever saw Luther Mallory laugh out loud.

The Wrong-Way Ambush

The Jeep took a bad bounce off a rock and Jim Hardy fought the wheel and grabbed simultaneously for the little .243 with its muzzle against the floorboard, trying to protect the scope.

The turkeys were running like ostriches, and he was dodging cactus and brush, trying to get to the top of the hill to give the boy the one chance he would have as they crossed the game trail ahead.

Mike was excited, holding on with both hands, eyes intent

on the brush. As the brakes screeched, he bailed out and Jim handed him the .243 and grabbed for the binoculars.

"Shoot only if you get a clear chance at one—don't cripple."

The turkeys were streaking across the trail, heads low and beards bobbing, and the last one, a young tom, hesitated a split second, just long enough for a snap shot. Then he was gone.

"Why didn't you shoot?"

"You said not to, unless I was sure," Mike said, lip beginning to tremble. "Can't I do anything right?"

Jim felt a light but stern shove at the back of his neck. Sara didn't assert herself often when hunting; this hunting was his big deal. But that little shove meant a lot; it meant to shut up and congratulate the boy on being a sportsman, not ask why he had not shot.

"You did exactly right," Jim said. "I guess the one I was looking at that stood there for a second was really out of sight to you; he was back in the brush."

The boy knew he was lying. The boy knew a lot of things about grownups that only a youngster who has grown up in a Boys' Home can know about grownups.

They drove on down the trail, slower and bouncing less, and Jim showed the boy the difference between a goat track and a deer track, and the soft, scratched-up dirt where the turkeys had been dusting themselves. The boy looked on politely but with the same distant, don't-put-me-on stare.

Sara had been right, as usual. Maybe it was too soon to take him hunting. The adoption had gone through only three weeks before, and there was a lot of getting acquainted to be done between a couple with no children for twelve years and a boy who'd been in trouble with the law before he was twelve. She knew how excited Jim got when somebody goofed on a deer or turkey or a covey rise on quail. The only time he'd ever yelled at her was the time she missed a standing shot at the big buck he'd rattled. But how could the boy know all that, and how could he understand all these things at once, a new home, a new thing entirely, this outdoors?

They rolled on down the hill, where the little dry creekbed

cut around the base of a steep bluff. If there would be one way to get a boy his first turkey, it would be to locate their roost.

In all his life, Jim had never hunted a turkey roost. Besides being poor sportsmanship, there was the possibility the turkeys would just leave the country. Even the Indians rarely hunted a roost; they knew that once a smart old tom is disturbed in his "bed" he might never use it again.

But Jim realized that somewhere in the back of his mind, right now, he was considering it for the first time. One of those big toms they'd seen today would be a trophy that could mean a whole lot of confidence to a boy in a brand-new environment, around new friends and grownups who lived, talked, and breathed hunting. It would be something to brag about to the other kids in school; plenty of them had killed deer already, but very few had even seen a wild turkey.

He watched the boy walking beside him, practicing the way Jim had told him to walk, heel down first and rolling on the balls of his feet forward to keep from clumping the ground and breaking too much brush. He was trying.

The bottom of the creekbed was soft sand, and they walked in it without a sound. Within thirty yards, under the largest trees, Jim found what he'd expected. Mingled with the fallen oak leaves were droppings, feathers, and under one tree several bronze-barred tailfeathers which said, as clearly as a sign, that this was the tree the gobblers were using.

Jim showed the boy the difference between the blue-gray plumage of the hens and the bronze-banded feathers of the gobblers, and how the gobblers invariably roost together in one tree, the hens in others, during the winter months.

He couldn't tell if the boy believed all that or not, and he thought how easy it would be to prove it to him, to get his confidence once and for all. They could just hide at the base of the trees and wait until dusk, and that tree would suddenly be swooshing and flapping full of gobblers. He had watched turkeys go to roost too many times through the binoculars; he knew how it would be.

After lunch beside a windmill, where the water gushed clear

and clean into a watering trough, the boy fell asleep on the ground, and they left him and walked down the hillside.

Jim was pondering hunting the roost, and Sara stopped him in midsentence. "You're going to teach him what a great white hunter you are and get his confidence by doing something that is exactly backwards to the sportsmanship you've been preaching to him since the first day? I think, Jim, that you're going to have to change a little along with the boy!"

At dusk that evening he and Mike were sitting back to back beside a small ravine high on the hill a quarter-mile from the roost. The turkeys would probably take off to fly to roost from the highest spot available, and this was it. On the other side of the hill, just in the off chance they came from that way, Sara was waiting with her .222.

The sun had started down behind the hill, and from somewhere across the trees there came the clear, musical "puut-puut" of a turkey hen.

The boy moved, shuffled himself into a more comfortable position against the tree, and Jim hissed a warning.

"You just can't move," he whispered. "A wild turkey has the finest eyesight in the woods."

The boy looked down, refusing to meet his gaze. This was it, the rebellion. He wasn't even looking at the hillside any more, just looking down, tracing a pattern into the dirt with a stick.

It was not the time to lecture patience, not to a product of an age when all a boy has to do to get action is to switch television channels or move to the next street corner.

"All right," Jim said evenly. "Get up and go back to the Jeep. Either that, or get yourself comfortable and don't make another move, don't even bat an eye. I mean it."

The boy looked down, but kept still.

Another fifteen minutes passed, and the chill of the night crept in. The sun was gone, the tops of the trees in the lowlands below tinted with the last rays.

Jim shuddered involuntarily. This was really it. The boy had stayed. Those turkeys had better come if he was ever to believe anything Jim said again.

Mike was in a better position to see them if they came down the draw, and suddenly he started to tremble, as a bird dog puppy trembles at the first scent of quail.

"Can you see their beards?" Jim whispered.

The boy moved only his lips. "They are making a parade," he whispered. "I can't see anything else."

Without a sound, a dark shadow moved between two trees, another shadow behind it. Jim focused his eyes upon the spot, and the third shadow stopped in the opening just long enough to

backlight against the sky the long, black beard waving like a tassel from his breast.

Suddenly there was a tremendous pounding and beating of wings and heavy black bodies were airborne, gliding down the hill toward the roost. Jim's heart sank. But then he remembered; hens go to roost first.

The gobblers suddenly reappeared out of the ravine, and it was now or never, dark objects moving in and out of the brush, too fast for any man to be sure of a kill.

Anything was worth a try, and Jim whispered for the boy to be ready, then whistled loud and clear, with his fingers in the corners of his mouth for volume.

The lead gobbler stopped in his tracks, neck craning, looking twice as large as the others. Jim could feel Mike tensing, sighting in on him. He knew the boy would take that big one . . . and Jim put the crosshairs carefully on a tom at the back of the bunch.

"On three," he whispered, "One, two," . . . blam!

Mike couldn't wait. The reverberating explosion shattered the canyon. Jim's turkey bolted to run, the .243 barked, and he went rolling and flapping in a shower of feathers. From the corner of his eye Jim could see the giant, lead gobbler rolling and tumbling down the side of the draw, a great, black rooster with his neck wrung.

Mike was right behind him, rifle forgotten, everything forgotten except a boy's shrillest, wildest yell . . . "I got him!"

Turkeys were running and taking off like B-29's out of the brush. But the sight of Mike, trying to tackle his flopping gobbler, was worth more than another gobbler.

"You made a fine shot on him," Jim said when things finally quieted down. "No meat ruined, right where I told you to shoot, where the neck joins the body."

"I just shot at the whole turkey," he admitted. "I don't really remember where I shot."

It was one of the biggest gobblers Jim had ever seen, an old patriarch of the brush country, iridescent in the fading light, with long sharp spurs that had whipped many a young gobbler in mating season, coarse hair beard looking a foot long on the rocks beside him.

"You carry yours," Mike said, "I'll carry mine."

He had to drag the big bird, because he couldn't get it over his shoulder. Jim let him drag it.

Mike was yelling at Sara before they got within three hundred yards of her. "You should have stayed with us," he yelled. "They came all around us, right where Jim said they would. I knew they would," he added, looking quickly at Jim.

That night, in front of a roaring campfire, with the last grill of venison backstrap cooking over the coals and Mike long since asleep inside the camp trailer, Jim pondered aloud why the turkeys had come from the wrong direction, absolutely the wrong way considering the wind.

"They didn't," he asked, "just happen to come by that draw where I left you, did they?"

She smiled, took a sip of nightcap, and put one finger to her lips.

He didn't have to ask why she didn't shoot. She'd spooked 'em straight over the boy.

"Even a great white hunter," she whispered, "has to be wrong once in a while."

Big Red's Buffleheads

Big Red Shayne was a bear of a man, six-four and barrel-chested, and it was said he'd been a mighty gambler with fists, dice, and ladies . . . and also that when the feds got too hot he'd just moved to Rockport with a suitcase full of cash and a shovel, and settled down to running the little bait camp.

The young reporter had heard all that, and more. A bookie in Houston had tipped him that there was a real exposé to be done on the wide-open gambling along the lower Texas coast, and that Big Red knew the score if anybody did.

So they sat with sunshine streaming in the window, looking over the bay, sizing each other up suspiciously. It had taken four beers to get to the point, and the reporter eased into it casually.

"Understand there's still a little action over at Port Aransas. Wonder how they get by with that, when Texas has been closed up tight for so long?"

Big Red looked him over, and wiped his mouth with the back of his hand.

"Well, Texas been closed to whorin', too, son," he rumbled, "but there ain't no shortage of puntang."

A commercial fisherman, weathered and weary from a night's netting, came in and bought a six-pack, and when Big Red came back to the table he brought two more cold beers.

"Son, you've got to realize things are a little different down here out of the way; sure, folks get by with a few things they couldn't in a city, maybe, but they have to make a livin' any way they can.

"Now you take ole Sonny Smith; he came home from the war all busted up, couldn't work a shrimp boat with one arm. But he knew the shrimpin' business, and he'd learned a few things in France.

"So he gets himself a speedboat, about the same hull they used to run rum out of Cuba, and he finds himself a couple of good-looking Mexican gals. Them shrimpers are mostly young, able-bodied men, and they stay out there a week at a time.

"Well, ole Sonny knew they shrimp all night, and sleep all day, and he'd sit around here listening to the marine radio. Soon as the skippers started wakin' up and talkin' to each other about noon, he'd take a fix on the fleet and head offshore with them girls.

"He'd come back in here with that little boat so loaded with Gulf shrimp she'd barely plane."

The reporter was writing as fast as his pencil would go, and Big Red noticed his beer was getting warm. "I'll finish that for you," he grumbled. "No use lettin' it get soapy."

"I'm not sure I understand," the reporter frowned.

"Well, son, he had a little rope ladder he could throw up on the shrimp boat, if the boys were a mind to have visitors; them Mexican gals could climb it like monkeys. He was smart enough to stay outside the ten-mile limit, which is international waters, and do his business. Ain't no laws against swappin' for shrimp, anyway. And in case you ain't bought any lately, that Gulf shrimp comes about as high as gold."

"You still haven't told me anything about gambling," the reporter said, getting bolder with the beer.

Big Red got up, pants hanging precariously under the parabolic paunch, and picked up a case of bottled beer out of the cooler with one hand.

"I figured," he said gruffly, "you'd as soon see it as hear about it; let's load up and take a little boat ride over toward Aransas."

They stepped out onto the rickety board pier into the sunshine, startled a couple of gulls sitting on the pilings, and the reporter had trouble with city-soft hands untying the heavy lines with the half-hitches Big Red had yanked into them.

The old 27-foot Chris Craft needed paint, and had green salt corrosion for fittings, but the engine started easily, and there was every evidence she'd made more than one trip across to Aransas lately.

They throbbed slowly out into the bay, Big Red obviously enjoying the beer and the bright afternoon sunshine.

"Over yonder," he waved to the east, "is the damnedest bunch of wild country you ever saw, not a soul except in boats from here to Port O'Connor, and that's close to fifty miles. Fine duck huntin' and fishin' back in there."

He nosed the boat toward the shoreline, where a drilling crew was setting up at the edge of the water, and piles of cable and pipe created the general impression of a rust-rotting junkyard.

"This Texas coast has to be the ugliest, junkiest place in the world," the reporter decided, speech slurred with the sixth beer.

"That all depends on who's lookin' at it, son. Now this here is my country. You see them little ducks, they're buffleheads, pretty little things. Now you watch 'em mind me."

He gunned the boat toward the ducks on the water, and bellowed at the top of his lungs. "Hey ducks, git up and go right over that rig yonder, and don't get more'n two feet off the water doin' it!"

The buffleheads taxied across the water, got airborne, flew two feet high over the oil rig and went down into the next cove.

"See, this is Big Red country," he rumbled, laughing from somewhere down deep in the beer belly, "and the best way to live and do well in it is to get along with Big Red."

They crossed into Lydia Ann Channel and met a succession of seagoing shrimpers inbound for Aransas Pass, crews jumping around on deck and hosing down for port, tanned, muscled men, dark from the sun and tough as rawhide. The reporter thought of the Mexican girls, and how they were bound to be tough as leather, too. Every passing boat left the heavy smell of diesel, dead fish, and rotting seaweed, and he guessed those Mexican girls used up a lot of perfume.

The waterfront of Port Aransas loomed ahead as a row of weathered boards and buildings dominated by Matthews Dock, high on its pilings, a combination tackle store, grocery, beer joint, and tourist perch big as a Coast Guard station, alabaster white in the afternoon sun, with gulls diving for garbage along the neat rows of fishing cruisers with sailfish flags fluttering from their outriggers.

Big Red nosed the boat up behind Wilson's Grill, and an old man came running down the dock to handle the lines.

"Now don't go causin' no ruckus in there," he grinned toothlessly at Big Red, "they're breakin' in two new boys on the crap table, and the girl dealin' blackjack can't pour pee out of a boot, but they're doin' all right. The boss's got some good help comin' from the Bahamas soon as the season's over down there."

Right then the reporter knew he had been traveling with a man not quite yet out of the gambling business.

They walked through the back door of the Tarpon Club, which was dark and cool inside, and the girl serving them was very pretty. The reporter wondered aloud what she could be doing in a little dive in Port Aransas.

"Hustlin'," Big Red grunted. "You see all those yachts tied up back of Matthews, and all them pretty homes along the front. Anywhere you see that, son, you'll find some pretty girls behind the bar."

"You mean they're all prostitutes?"

"No, they're barmaids," Big Red chuckled, a rumbling from down deep that erupted into a spell of coughing and throat-clearing.

The reporter felt Red's hamlike hand below the bar, giving him a crisp bill. "Pay for the drinks with that," he grinned, "and see what happens."

It was a hundred-dollar bill, and the girl's eyes came alive. "Look at that Texas calling card," she cooed, patting the reporter's hand on the bar. "Now you're gonna take every cent of my change. I'll have to go next door, be right back."

Big Red winked at him.

She came back shortly, and behind her was an even more beautiful girl of perhaps twenty, in slacks and gold harem slippers, who dropped two quarters into the juke box and sat down at the end of the bar.

Big Red stood up, belched, and walked out through the front door with the little one-way glass peephole in it. "Let that be a lesson to you," he rumbled. "That little sweetheart in there would have fresh meat like you in there rollin' dice in fifteen minutes."

The street was like the set of some Western movie, a row of high-fronted buildings, wide and with no cars except a few parked here and there to the side, and tourists walking down the middle of the street gaping and taking snapshots.

They stepped into the green felt dimness of the Sportsman's Club, passed a couple of pool tables and the bar, back through a swinging door into a carpeted room with a long crap table and a noisy ring of players. The croupier gave Big Red an acknowledging look as he called the point.

A florid-faced man with a drink walked up and slapped Big Red on the back, started mumbling something about the last time he saw him, and Big Red eased on over to the side door and back out into the street.

"Damn drunks wart the hell out of me," he grumbled. "Let's go eat something and wait until they get through shearing them sheep in there."

Wilson's Grill was a pretty place, with big photographic murals of local scenes, mostly shrimp boats and beaches, blown up large as life on the walls, and the backs of the chairs and Negro waiters were all in white jackets.

The reporter couldn't figure such an elite restaurant in such a small fishing town.

"Same deal as them pretty girls next door," Big Red mused. "It's a part of the deal, boy; gamblers know how to lay on the good stuff. Strong as they run these games, they can lose on the food."

"If the games are so tight to make that much overhead, why will people play?"

"Not all the buffleheads in this world are out on that bay, son."

Two yacht skippers came in, tanned and owlish under the eyes where the sunglasses had cut the Gulf glare, looking healthy and crisply clean in white. Behind them were three wealthy-looking couples in fishing clothes.

One of the guides recognized Big Red and came over to the table.

"Come to look over the store?" he grinned. "Looks like you're all doin' all the good; the Sportsman is jumpin' over there. You come down to rattle a few bones with the old pro?" he asked the reporter.

"Naw," Big Red chuckled, "he's gettin' ready to write himself a big newspaper story, and he wants to find out all about this illegal gamblin' goin' on right under the eyes of the law."

"Oh, I see," winked the skipper. "Whatever became of that reporter that was over here a couple of years ago to do that? Can't say I ever heard about him since. Maybe he misspelled Mafia or something."

They laughed, finished the beer, and it was all the reporter could do to force down the last swallows.

They shoved off with the sun going down over behind Matthews, the old Chris laboring all she could do to get back across the bay before dark.

The reporter watched the neon signs disappear in the distance, knowing this was one story he would never write, and also that that had been exactly why Big Red brought him over in the first place.

But it wouldn't have made much difference, anyway, because Hurricane Carla blew right in through that pleasant little sin alley, with the howling wrath of an avenging angel, taking with her the weathered waterfront and possibly Big Red, too, because he died right afterward in his sleep, as if this cleaned-up coast was too dull a place now. Matthews Dock had turned into a bustling business center, the gamblers were gone, and the girls behind the bars were serving cokes and beer and not nearly so pretty as they used to be.

But the buffleheads are still here, every fall and late into the spring, skimming low over the water . . . just as they did a thousand years before Big Red told them to.

The Sand Trout Seminar

The fifty-foot crew boat *Molly Sue* shuddered and groaned as the big diesels swung her stern parallel to the South Galveston jetty.

Bob Campbell watched carefully over the bow, then gave the signal for the anchor. The skipper complied grudgingly. He didn't like to be told how to fish, not on his own boat anyway.

Down below, in the air-conditioned salon, the old man was holding forth at gin rummy, cigar jutting the angle of his craggy chin, eyes as sharp for the cards as when he dealed and wheeled into his empire of oil fifty years before.

"Who is the guy up there telling old Joe what to do?" one of the legislators asked, flicking a grain of sand from impeccable white deck shoes. "You reckon it's smart having an outsider along when we're trying to talk business?"

The old man marked up some points on the scorepad and gave the legislator a sudden, incisive glance. "If I want laws passed I call you boys," he said, "and if I want to entertain some folks on a fishing trip, I call Bob Campbell."

The legislator reddened slightly around the ears, and observed that this was certainly the prettiest crew boat he'd ever seen.

"Uncle Sam thinks it's a crew boat," the old man said dryly. "I think it's a yacht."

Up on deck the fishermen lining the rail were mostly pale and paunchy, with the sedentary gray look around the jowls which comes from too many late conferences.

Campbell glanced up at them occasionally, from picking out backlashes and rigging tackle, and decided lawmakers and lobbyists are pretty much alike, and also that he was glad that he didn't have to make a living that way.

Silvery sand trout began flying through the air and flopping on deck with monotonous regularity; Campbell had anchored perfectly for the lines to go straight down beside the base of the granite jetties into the deep hole he knew was there.

One of the younger legislators, more interested in cold beer than the sand trout, asked how he knew exactly where to anchor, when other boats all around were catching nothing.

"You just have to understand fish, and when they're in one spot or another in relation to the tide," Campbell explained. "This jetty fishing is changing all the time, just like the whole coast, and most people don't fish enough to realize it."

"You say the coast is changing," another legislator said. "Looks like we're doing pretty well fishing, yet all we hear from the sportsmen is that pollution and netting and all sorts of things are ruining the coast."

Campbell carefully impaled two pieces of cut bait on the hook of a gray-faced senator from inland, and wiped his hands on the white towel at his belt.

"There's a little more to it than that," he said. "These are gulf trout; I could take you up where we used to catch most of our fish in Trinity and upper Galveston Bay, and you couldn't get a bite in a week. Drag a shrimp trawl in there, and you'll come up with a stinking, oily mess about like molasses except that you can barely stand to dump it out of the net without throwing up; the whole bay bottom is that way up there."

"So, what's that got to do with out here?"

Campbell wearily wiped his hands and opened a beer.

"Well, I guess you guys that make the laws really couldn't have time to know all this stuff, but looks like you'd at least get some advice from the game and fish people. The whole life cycle of shrimp, trout, redfish and a whole lot more depends upon the upper bays. Those are the nursery grounds where the baby shrimp, and also the little fish, grow up, and when we lose those to pollution there won't be much seafood or fishing on this coast."

The man from Parks and Wildlife had listened intently from the rail, and he reeled in and joined the growing group around the beer box.

"Our department has to keep itself as far removed from politics as possible," he said coolly. "If we are asked an opinion on pollution or some such thing we have our experts in that field answer it in written form, documented by our own research. But we can't go around telling the legislature what to do."

"Then it's not your job to inform someone whether or not some tragedy is about to occur to the resources you're supposed to be protecting? You might feel the need of telling 'em, for instance, that these new saltwater barriers and the new water diversion plan is going to rob the coast of the proper salinity for oyster and fish production."

Campbell was chopping cut bait as he talked, the knife swift and sure from years of cleaning fish.

"This idea of moving water from East Texas, where we

have too much at times, over to West Texas, where they never have enough, really sounds good," he was saying, stopping to take a sip of beer. "But when you look at it another way, you begin to wonder if there isn't some better way to get irrigation water out west, without ruining the whole ecology of the coastal bays."

"I don't understand at all," a young legislator broke in. "What I hear is that freshwater floods kill off the oyster beds and drive out the saltwater fish. And now we propose a way to divert that freshwater, and you say it's going to ruin the coast?"

"That's right," said Campbell, "because there has to be a certain amount of fresh water coming into the upper bays to reduce the salinity and make oysters, shrimp, and everything else grow properly. You ever fish the Laguna Madre between Corpus and Port Isabel? No. I thought not. Well, for your information, since there is so little freshwater runoff in there any more, the oysters are all gone; they can't live in such high salinity, and for that matter, fish and shrimp can't do as well, either, particularly in their early development."

"Say," said the young legislator, "that's quite a speech for a deckhand."

Campbell's face flushed beneath the tan.

The old man had come up from below, blinking in the bright sunlight like a wizened owl, and he had heard the last remark.

"Never did get around to introducing all you boys to Mr. Campbell," he said. "Bob has a degree from A&M, flew jets in World War II, and I expect reads more than most of you boys do now. But he just likes to fish, and I'm not so sure from the looks of him and the looks of you that he doesn't have something there."

One of the older legislators, who had been in the card game and who obviously stayed close to the old man's side, asked Campbell what he would do about such problems as pollution.

"You imply we're not doing our job, and Parks and Wildlife isn't doing theirs," he said. "What would you do, just shut down the industries which have built this state, discourage all the new ones planning to come in, and send them over to Louisiana or some competitive state where they don't yet have tough pollution controls? You, and a lot of people like you, Mr. Campbell, need to remember that this world is not just a bowl of cherries set up for the sportsmen . . . we're in a day-to-day battle for existence with other states and with foreign manufacturers where there are no guaranteed wages nor expensive pollution control laws. If we put in the kind of pollution controls you sportsmen would like to have, the state and most of its industries would be out of business in a year! There isn't a city in all of Texas that wouldn't go bankrupt if it had to suddenly build the completely adequate sewage disposals that would eliminate even that form of pollution. It just isn't that simple a question, and it's time you sportsmen realized there's more to it than just shutting off some big valve."

"So what will we have unless somebody does shut off the valve?" Campbell said evenly. "How long will it be before new industries won't come in here because their personnel won't live in polluted air and polluted water? How long will it be before a lot of other industries just wither away?"

"Such as which industries?"

"Such as the number one industry in Texas last year in dollar volume, tourism, and such as the seafood industry, the resort and sport fishing industry, and the related industries which depend upon them."

The man from Parks and Wildlife broke in and asked if Campbell had heard about the new survey getting underway to determine the relative value of game, fish and recreational resources to the state.

"I've heard about a good many surveys," he answered. "So many surveys on pollution, for instance, that by the time one is finished it's obsolete, and another one has to be started. I don't see much more sense in wasting money surveying the value of game, fish and recreation when we already know it is valuable, than there is in surveying pollution when we already know it's killing this coast. I wonder if surveys sometimes aren't the only sure way to make sure nothing is going to be done to rock the boat for a while."

The senator stiffened.

"Unfortunately for this state, no one with the responsibility nor capability for these much-needed changes seems to be nearly so smart as you are, Mr. Campbell, or others of you who do very little more about the problems than to bitch about them. I suggest you get yourself elected to the legislature, so that you can personally straighten this state out."

The old man raised his hand, and told Campbell there'd been enough fishing for one day. The legislators and game and fish people went below with him into the air conditioning.

That night, with Campbell and the skipper off the boat, and scotch replacing the beer, blue smoke hovered over the card table in more serious swirls and the old man was in complete command.

"Now you boys see what we're going to be up against this session, and don't discount these sportsmen . . . they're from all social levels, there are tens of thousands of them, and they have some sensible points to make."

"But so do we," said the senator.

"That's right, we all do, and we've got to keep this state going and growing, just as we have all these years. Which is exactly why I had Bob Campbell on the boat today. The only way we can do that is to know what arguments we're up against in advance."

"What if all he says is true?" asked the young representative. "What if this pollution and all finally reaches the saturation point and begins to kill off a lot of other industries besides yours?"

The old man looked at him sharply, quickly, and shuffled the cards.

"That," he said, "will be for someone else to worry about. Right now I'd suggest you worry about your next term . . . Now sit down and I'll give you another little lesson called gin."

Grandfather's Geese

Low, gray fog hung in drapes and billows over the glassy lagoon between Seadrift and Port O'Connor, but somewhere above it the peeping whistles and swishing of wings meant that the pintails were flying, and that the sun would burn through.

Suddenly six giant bodies came hurtling out of the mist, scarcely higher than the duck blind, and were gone, leaving the clear, melodious call of the Canada goose hanging in the fog behind them.

"Maybe you better pinch me," said Brooks Davis. "There isn't a wild goose that big in this hemisphere!"

Stu Walters was staring at the mist where the huge birds had disappeared, trying to bring back something from far back in his mind. "I always figured the old man was just makin' up another tall tale for us kids," he mused, "but I distinctly remember my grandfather telling us about some giant geese down in this country someplace where he used to hunt fifty years ago. Way he told it, they were sort of ghost geese, smarter than people. Said he killed one once, and the thing looked up at him with such a human expression he never bothered 'em again."

That night at the little café on the Intracoastal Canal, other hunters made sport out of Brooks' story about the big geese, and Stu suggested they had probably been fooled by the fog which makes things look farther away than they are, and thus larger.

But when they stepped outside, an old, gray-bearded commercial fisherman followed them, bringing with him wafts of stale perspiration and unwashed old age.

"Might know somethin' about them big geese," he said in a cracked falsetto. "You boys got a beer?"

"Naw, you fellers ain't crazy," he cackled after three memory courses. "Them geese is out there right now, roostin' somewhar over toward Panther Point where nobody goes. Ain't many of 'em, never was. But they been there forever."

Stu was racking his brain, trying to remember places his grandfather had mentioned.

"Is there someplace around here called Steamboat Pass?" he asked.

The old man looked at him quickly. "Now I ain't heard that name called in many a year," he said. "Nowadays they call it South Pass. Sure, son, it's right down the canal here, and that's exactly where I seen them big geese the first time.

"Used to have me some redfish lines way back toward the end of the lagoon, and I'd see them rascals near about every day, crossin' way out over the bay. Once when it was slick calm I run down the Intracoastal fur enough to git a good look, and them dang things seen me and moved on over another half mile, me jest sittin' there in the skiff without no gun."

"How many of them did you see?" Brooks pressed.

"Dunno, maybe fifty or sixty at the most. They come acrost in little bunches, sometimes pairs, and be my guess they feed up in that turrible marsh and saltgrass country 'tween here and the new game refuge over on Blackjack."

"What makes you think so?"

"'Cause there ain't no way for man ner animal to git in thar at 'em; a man'd sink outa sight in that bog."

Stu and Brooks looked at each other. Obviously the old man hadn't seen the new airboat they'd brought in from the Louisiana marsh country. With its 125-horsepower Lycoming aircraft engine, it could run on a heavy dew.

The next morning they cruised down the Intracoastal Canal to the entrance of San Antonio Bay, and let the boat drift along the desolate shoreline. Pintails buzzed the shallow lagoon, and Stu wished they'd brought some duck decoys, just in case the old man had been making up the whole story of the giant geese.

Far across the bay, through the binoculars, he could see white dots on the sandbars at the edge of the Aransas National Wildlife Refuge, pelicans probably, or possibly whooping cranes. The rare cranes often feed along the sides of the Intracoastal, and he and Brooks had seen them up close, strange white birds with seven-foot wingspreads and gangling long legs, the last of their kind. He wondered why the giant Canada geese did not also use the sanctuary of the refuge.

Brooks was watching the other direction, and suddenly he grabbed for the binoculars. Stu followed his gaze and there was no mistaking them, dark silhouettes far over the bay, low to the water, giant wings beating slowly and powerfully against the north wind.

Stu cranked the Lycoming and nosed the airboat out of the canal and onto the shallow mudflats, angling the bow with the geese to take a compass bearing on their direction. Then he shoved the throttle and the little boat picked up and planed off. The chase was on!

An airboat can run faster over shallow water or mud than deep water, because shallow water cannot compress and gives more lift to the hull. But Stu pondered the chances he was taking; if an airboat comes out of wet mud and hits dry sand it can stop instantly, and at fifty miles an hour the G-forces could send that whirling prop and heavy engine through them as a fan through tissue paper.

But the geese were gaining, fighting the wind, and he shoved the throttle forward. Wind tears blurred their vision, and they didn't see a tiny spot of dry sand until too late; the boat shuddered, stuck for an instant, and then through sheer momentum jumped across and was gone again.

Stu glanced triumphantly at Brooks, and began shoving the boat mercilessly, relying on speed and momentum, feeling her jolt and bounce across the mud and wet sand of the points, salt-grass clumps whisking past on either side as they followed the narrow, winding course of a slough. They crossed a shallow mud flat, and the boat picked up speed, the tachometer climbing toward the red line, wind whistling in their ears and eyes.

Abruptly the bottom beneath the bow changed from greenish muck to brown mud, and a narrow sandbar in that instant became a low island. They felt the boat lurch wildly, climbing bow-high into the air and throwing Stu forward into the throttle. The big engine bellowed, the hull for a split second gained altitude as an overpowered-plane flying without wings, then slowly twisted in midair with the torque of the propeller and came down with a gut-jolting, smashing crunch into the sand.

Stu felt himself thrown clear, and the world spun wildly and smashed up into his face. Somewhere he heard Brooks curse, realized he was conscious and that he could move his arms and legs. His face was warm and wet, and he knew his nose was bleeding. Brooks was dragging himself to the boat, and when he shut off the screaming engine, there was in the sudden silence the mocking mellow cry of geese over their heads. Stu rolled over in the jumble of guns and equipment, feeling for broken bones, and sat up on one elbow looking at them. Then he grabbed for the binoculars on the sand beside him.

"We've found 'em," he yelled above the roaring in his head. "Look!"

The geese were slanting into a low glide, and directly ahead of them, less than a quarter mile away, was a clean spit of sand in the saltgrass prairie with the dark bodies and craning necks of many Canadas clearly outlined against it.

Brooks was stumbling to his feet, half dazed, and Stu saw the boat was high aground, but apparently not damaged. It would be two hours until the next high tide could possibly bring in enough water to free her.

"In other words," he thought out loud, "the logical thing to do is go hunting."

"Yeah," grinned Brooks. "Right now that is about the only thing to do."

More geese were passing over in small flights, a few Lesser Canadas flying with the giants and looking more like ducks by comparison. The trick would be to get near enough to the main concentration to get under some flight lowering to land. And to do it without spooking the whole bunch, they'd have to crawl.

It was easy at first, with hard sand under them. But then they were in thick clumps of sawgrass, each infested with its own hatch of mosquitos, and the dank, sour-smelling marsh that broke through into oozing mud beneath them.

Brooks was reaching out for a high spot to put one hand when he heard the bone-chilling buzzing of a rattlesnake. He froze, slowly turned his head, saw the grass move ever so slightly in the clump of saltgrass even with his left ear, and instantly rolled over and came up with his gun.

Stu saw it all and hissed a warning. "Don't shoot, you'll spook the whole bunch!"

He was already crawling on ahead, cradling the gun in both arms, walking on elbows, using the gun barrel to probe each salt-grass clump ahead for rattlers.

They were almost in position when the yodeling of Canadas came downwind and close.

Stu parted a clump of saltgrass and saw them coming head-on, six feet above the ground, huge wings slow but powerful against the wind.

"Don't come up until I call the shot," Stu whispered. "We'll get one chance and that'll be it."

Two giants loomed low over the saltgrass, so close their black chinstraps, straining wing pinions, even the mud on their feet, were clearly visible as they passed over.

Stu let them go; six more were behind them.

They came ever so slowly, and when they were directly overhead, Stu and Brooks fought the urge to look up, burying noses in the stinking marsh, and a few feet over their ears the geese let out a clamor of greeting calls to the main concentration.

Stu's grandfather had told him many years before how to wait out geese in a gale, to hold fire until the big birds were going dead away, where the feathers were most vulnerable to the shot, and where they would have to flare back downwind over the gun.

Brooks watched Stu, saw him gathering his feet under him, and when the geese were twenty-five yards past them, lowering flaps, he yelled, and they both came up together. The huge white rumps were almost on a line with their guns, big black feet starting down.

As he brought the barrel into line with them, Stu tried to concentrate on centering the load in the biggest gander. With the first shot he saw the bird wince and come staggering back with the wind. The gun swung ahead of the black head of another huge goose, back-flaring and climbing, and white tailfeathers spurted on the first shot. He swung up and farther ahead of the straining, outstretched neck, and the huge shape crumpled. The first goose was in a power dive, powerful wings still beating as he crashed into the marsh with a heavy whopping splash and bounced up again in a shower of feathers.

Subconsciously he heard Brooks' double fire twice and felt the heavy thud of a giant body into the sand beside him.

The noise of the shooting had put the concentration into the air, great birds clamoring majestically and circling their centuries-old haven in confusion. And suddenly Stu felt a strange sensation, as if somewhere above the low bank of clouds to the north, his grandfather might be up there shaking his head.

These were, after all, the old man's geese. They were like him, bigger and wiser than life, refusing to live under the doting care of the government . . . staying to themselves just as the old man always had.

Stu walked over and picked up the great gander which had fought so valiantly to stay aloft, an old gray-and-black patriarch with a wingspread wider than he could reach, feathers ruffling in death by the north wind.

"Let's leave 'em alone for now," he said softly, stroking a strange patch of white in front of the bird's bill which he had never seen before on a Canada goose.

"If we disturb 'em again right here, they may move and we'd never find 'em again."

Brooks was watching the last of the big geese disappear on the horizon. "Yeah," he said, "and if we don't get a trench dug up to the boat by high tide, we're liable to be livin' right here with 'em."

That night in town, still muddy and in hunting clothes, they dug out the bird books from Stu's library, and searched three of them before they came across the painting of the huge Canadas. There, unmistakably, was the strange white patch in front of the bill, the huge size.

Beneath the sketch the description read *"Branta canadensis maxima,* largest of the Canada geese, last sighted in 1922, and now extinct."

"Well, I'll be damned," Brooks whistled. "Are you thinking what I'm thinking?"

Stu nodded. "Now," he said softly, "I know why the old man never told anyone where they were. Brooks, you raise your right hand and solemnly swear after me . . ."

The Golden Redfish

The surface was a rose-orange reflection of the sky upon which the two fishermen, the old blue heron and the guide, were silhouetted statues watching the shallow flats come alive with the sunrise.

Forrest Jackson had passed up breakfast to get here early; if the redfish were here he wanted to find them and get out early, ahead of the tourists. These redfish could be his future if they would just cooperate.

He moved slowly, sliding each step across the soft marl bottom as a precaution against stingrays and also to avoid any bottom-jarring jolts. A spooky redfish could feel that as easily as Jackson could hear the dull boom of the surf at Pass Cavallo or the coarse, startled croak of the old heron.

These things he understood; all his life he had fished and guided. But times were changing, and someday he would be an old man. He needed to build something for the wife and kids, something that would be there when he could guide no more. And these redfish, this day, just might turn the trick.

Across the flat, the gaunt, hollow shell of the old Coast Guard station rose above the blending mirage of water and horizon, long abandoned for more protected quarters on the mainland. Port O'Connor was changing, suddenly developing into a tourist center after a sleepy century as a quiet little fishing village.

Now there was the new ship channel into the Gulf, built for the fast-developing industries at the upper end of the big bay, offering for the first time easy access to the Gulf for the big sport fishing boats, bringing in new Gulf current and new life for the back bays, improving even the trout and redfish fishing for which the area had become famous.

The tourists were coming by the thousands now, trailering in their own boats, jamming the launching ramps, swarming the little waterfront café. Now was the time to make his move, if he ever made it.

He cast effortlessly, using the stiff, two-handed popping rod's handle for leverage, letting the little gold spoon probe the lip of the flat where it dropped off into the deep channel leading into Saluria Bayou. He kept the rod high and reeled fast to hold the flashing lure just above the grassy bottom.

The tide was flooding in strong, mullet moving with it, surface-bulging schools darting and flashing in the sun, soon to be within range of the "long Tom" waiting so patiently on the shoreline. Jackson wondered how the old heron knew when the tide would come in; he had no tide tables, but he knew.

The spoon came wagging back, a will-o'-the-wisp flash darting here and there, much like a frightened mullet's side flashing in the sun. And suddenly it disappeared in a bronze swirl, the rod bucked with the splashing, exploding strike, and redfish panicked across the flat, purplish, bull-headed V-wakes, sending mullet leaping in silver, rainbow arcs ahead of them.

He found himself talking out loud to the redfish. "Take it easy, old boy, I need you. You and me are goin' to get that banker down here tomorrow for sure!"

Jackson had guided the man for years, and when he'd finally gotten up nerve to mention some land that might be available for a new resort and marina, the banker had right away asked if he would be interested in running such an operation. They'd talked about it casually at first, and then both became more excited as they realized how profitable it could be. Jackson was honest; the banker knew that as only two men can know each other from fishing together, and he also knew that Jackson could handle the myriad mechanics of running such a place; he'd spent his life working around them.

For the restaurant, Liz would be just about perfect. She was an excellent cook, had her own café when Jackson met her, and she knew how to get along with the natives who would comprise the kitchen help as well as the tourists who would be the customers.

But the banker had been worried. Pollution, overfishing by nets and many other factors were seriously starting to affect the Texas coast. Already the smoke of more industry was hovering over the horizon. Could the fishing hold up well enough, long enough to pay out the tremendous investment? Would small boat fishermen, the bread and butter of the resort business, turn inland toward the huge new freshwater reservoirs built by Uncle Sam?

Jackson had told him how much the new pass had improved the fishing, but every time the banker had come to fish the weather had been poor. Now they were at the point of decision. The option on the land along the Intracoastal had to be exercised or dropped. The banker had to be convinced. And Jackson figured this one school of redfish would convince anybody if he could pin them down. Now he could make that one, vital phone call to Houston.

The red streaked off across the flat in his last, sweeping run, the arc of the line gathering floating grass from the surface into a bundle which slid down as the fish fought, so that when Jackson picked him up finally, it was much like unpacking a golden-bronze trophy from excelsior.

Swiftly, but quietly, Jackson strung the fish and dipped his right hand in the cool water; one bit of slime on the handle of the rod would make it difficult to hold. And he could see the tails of three more redfish waving at the surface in front of him as they rooted bottom, more of the school which had not spooked. As he straightened up, slowly and carefully, he saw more bulging wakes moving across the flat.

He took his time, waited for the tails to disappear, because then the redfish would have their heads up to see the spoon, and pitched a short cast in front of them. Instantly, purplish-bronze streaks exploded around him and the reel screeched off line. This one was bigger, he figured about ten pounds, just perfect for light tackle.

Suddenly he heard the drone of the little airplane, and instantly threw the reel out of gear and let the fish take line, leaving his rod straight as if there was nothing on it. But he knew then it had been too late.

The plane was the "spotter" for a local group of part-time netters, and with the water clear, the pilot could see that school of redfish much better than Jackson could. The plane circled repeatedly, assaying the size of the school and the size of the fish.

Suddenly, Jackson felt an unrealized hatred welling up within him. These bays had been closed to netting for years, to give the game fish a chance. Yet everyone around Port O'Connor knew who was doing the netting by night, everyone knew about the spotter plane. Even the game warden knew it. But there was nothing any of them seemed to be able to do about it.

Twice the warden had caught the netters in the act, and both times the local justice of the peace, and ultimately the judge of the county, had given such low fines that it had gotten to be a local joke.

Jackson knew most of the full-time commercial netters, and he understood their side. They had to live, too. But they were no longer the problem. Most of them had taken jobs with the new industries springing up along the coast for better pay and a lot less work. The problem now was the netters who really didn't have to net, who did it for part-time fun, or spending money, or perhaps mostly to brag about in the little café where the game warden could hear them and get up and walk out with his ears red and his face flushed.

There were still redfish around him, but Jackson took no more chances. He waded slowly and quietly back to the boat, threw the two fish into it and headed for home.

Now he knew it would be a gamble. The reds were there, and they would be there if the weather held. The gamble was whether the netters would move in on them tonight. He thought of calling the warden, and then he thought again. A man's house could burn down, or his boat could sink. The netters had been there longer than he had, and they still felt Port O'Connor was theirs.

He made the call to Houston, did not mention the netters because time was running out on that land option, and went to bed early, turning and tossing in the darkness and hearing the throbbing diesels of towboats on the canal and seeing their flashing lights against the window curtains far into the night.

It was all so simple. Why couldn't the netter with the drive-in or the netter with the store see what they were doing, not just to him, but to the whole community? Left alone, that one school of redfish could bring tourists for weeks; the papers would report a big catch or two, and here would come the tourists and fishermen, leaving $500 in Port O'Connor for every redfish any of them would ever take home. The whole town would benefit, including the netters. Yet, somehow, he could not call the warden, and for the first time in his life he wondered if he was a coward.

The next morning dawned clear, with no wind, and the banker drove up to the dock sleepy-eyed and tired from the three-hour push from Houston.

"What'd you do, fight some beer joint all night?" the banker needled. "You look like you haven't slept a wink."

Jackson grinned, and nosed the little boat out of the basin and hit Little Mary's Cut at full throttle.

His hopes rose as they neared the Coast Guard flats. The tide was coming in strong now, the water was calm and not too clear, which was better still, because redfish hit better when it was not too clear.

It was when he turned into Saluria Bayou, and idled slowly and quietly into the spot he liked to park the boat, that he suddenly felt the overpowering urge to retch.

Along the shoreline, in the grass where the old heron had stood, were the unmistakable signs of the netters; small piles of grass from the flat that had been swept ashore in the mesh, the tracks of the men who had walked the muddy shoreline in the darkness with the big net between them.

It had happened exactly as he had envisioned through the night, the long gill net stretched across the flat, the men wading the water, pounding the surface with paddles, driving the reds in terror for deeper water, and into the tangling web of the net.

The banker wanted to fish anyway, and they waded until the tide quit running. They caught three small redfish, survivors of the massacre the night before, and Jackson saw his hopes for the marina, and perhaps for Port O'Connor, gradually fade in the old man's eyes.

That afternoon they drove over to the commercial fish house and saw them, the long bins of the icehouse overflowing with them, bronze beauties to nearly twenty pounds, still fresh and glowing golden in the dim light.

"Yeah, they really mopped up on 'em last night," the old man with the shovel said, as he began loading fish from one bin into another, separating them by size for shipment. "Claim they got 'um down toward Matagorda, but most of 'um was still alive when they come in this mornin'," he grinned. "I bet the game warden turned over in his sleep last night."

"How much," asked the banker, "are they worth a pound?"

"Well, we're so loaded right now we ain't gettin' but twenty-seven cents."

The banker shook his head and they walked out into the brilliant sunlight, crunching the oyster shell underfoot and smelling the stench of the fish house.

"I think," the banker said, "we'd better just forget our project; if you want to work out something with somebody else, I'll help any way I can."

Jackson shook his head, suddenly feeling dry in the mouth and very sick to his stomach.

"No thanks," he said lightly. "I guess I wasn't supposed to be nothin' but a fishin' guide, anyway."

That night he drank beer until he could hold no more, and he had trouble climbing the steps to the house, because he knew she would be in there crying and he couldn't face her.

And all night long he dreamed of redfish of pure and solid gold.

The Whitewing Snow Job

Somewhere behind the stately row of palms shotgun fire crackled sporadically.

"Flight's starting," Jerry Crawford observed, watching the sky behind the old irrigation well where he and Burt Harter had taken shooting positions. "Reckon we should get back up in the brush a little?"

Burt shrugged. "Supposed to be a hundred thousand hunters

in the Rio Grande Valley today. I reckon by the time any birds get to us they'll be pretty well used to people with guns."

The horizon was etched with dark dots and long, low flight lines of doves almost as large as pigeons, rising and falling with the wind, looking deceptively slow as they fought the wind on their afternoon feeding flight.

"I expect this was sort of the way the old passenger pigeons looked in the old days," Jerry said, watching the spectacle.

"Yeah," said Burt, "which is probably why there aren't any more passenger pigeons."

A squadron of gray streaks came hurtling past, wing chevrons flashing white in the afternoon sun, and dived for the brush in the instant they saw the hunters.

Burt swung with the leader, followed his twisting flight through the low brush, and was starting to touch the trigger when he saw the movement and at the last instant raised the gun.

"Thank you very much," said a voice with a slight Spanish accent. "I think maybe we owe you a cold beer."

The tall, mustached man stepping out of the brush was carrying a folding stool and beer cooler, looking aristocratically cool in a tailored safari jacket and also vaguely familiar to Jerry.

"Aren't you from San Antonio?" he asked, sticking out his hand.

"Oh no," smiled Raul Ramirez, "I am a rare creature here today, a Mexican entertaining some guests with a dove shoot in your country. Usually it is the other way around."

"Don't we know it," Burt groaned, accepting a cold beer. "If it wasn't for all these so-called American sportsmen going across into Mexico and shooting everything that moves, we'd have whitewing flights in Texas like we used to have twenty years ago."

Raul shrugged, the polite way to disagree south of the border, and pointed out a couple of whitewings loafing along low over the brush. Suddenly both birds dropped, having blundered into a cluster of hunters behind the levee.

"You see," said Raul, "not all the whitewings get killed in

Mexico. In my lifetime of hunting in Mexico I have not seen so many hunters as I have seen in one afternoon here today."

The flight was thickening, thousands of birds streaking across the sky, and the hunters were firing as fast as they could load. Burt and Jerry finished their limits and came back to the shade, where Raul was already picking his birds.

He held up one of the picked doves, its body yellow with fat from the abundant grain of the Valley.

"It is a strange thing," he observed. "These birds have more than they can eat; their food is everywhere in the brush and now in the fields. Yet they are in such danger because man does not understand their real enemy."

Now Jerry remembered him; he'd been Mexico's delegate to an international conference on migratory birds a couple of years back.

"So what is their real enemy?" Burt wanted to know.

"The bulldozer," said Raul, "and the plow."

"I don't see many people running over whitewings today with bulldozers," Burt observed.

"No," Raul said, "but the reason you have fewer birds in the Rio Grande Valley than you had a few years ago is because so much of your land has been cleared, and their nesting places are disappearing. And also a few years ago, you had most of the small grain fields on the American side of the river; now we have so much grain in Mexico it is no longer necessary for the big migrations to come so far north to find grain."

"So what happened to the passenger pigeons?" Burt argued.

"The same thing that is now happening to the whitewing. The passenger pigeon's food and cover on his migrations was in the hardwood timber of your northern country, and as it fell to the axe the bird could not adapt to the change. He became easy prey to many predators, of which man was only one."

A couple of bankers from Philadelphia who were being entertained by Raul finally finished their limits and came up the dusty road.

"You guys amaze me," one said, mopping sweat-soaked hair

out of his eyes. "The rest of the country would like to have your bird problems; I've never seen so many gol-darned birds in my life!"

"I have just decided," Raul said, "you must come to my ranch in Tamaulipas and let us show you some whitewings."

"Fine," said Burt, "much obliged. We'll have to do that sometime."

"No," said Raul, "right now. The ranch is not more than ninety minutes from here in my plane, and there are only three of us. My friends from the north have business to attend to."

Burt looked at Jerry, who shrugged.

"You haven't had too many of those *cervezas* to fly that plane, have you?"

"The plane flies herself on automatic pilot under such circumstances," Raul grinned. "But we have to hurry, because I think the clouds will be closing in over the mountains."

Two hours later, they were low over the thick green jungle with the sun going down, and the ceiling lowering fast. Wisps of mist obscured the horizon and they were in a fast shrinking world of dripping, green jungle with gray rain streaking the windshield.

"A little more of this," suggested Jerry, "and I'd be heading for the beach."

"Oh, yes," Raul shrugged, "because I think there is a very big mountain near here."

The plane plowed into a wall of clouds and Burt instinctively ducked, as if the mist were the side of a mountain, and when they broke out again there was a cluster of native buildings below and a mowed stretch of green pasture beside the jungle. Raul threw the plane into a heart-stopping bank, sideslipped down between two tall palms, and a barbed-wire fence flashed under them so close Burt felt sure the wheels rolled across the top wire before they bounced into the pasture.

They stepped out of the plane into the warm, humid air of another more tranquil world. Quail were whistling around the airstrip and a flight of ducks passed over the river in front of the big, whitewashed adobe ranch house.

"Pato Real," said Raul, "the king of ducks. They are almost

as big as geese, and they live here all year. They land in trees. We have also the *Pa Chee Chee,* which is a smaller duck I believe you call the Fulvous Tree Duck."

They stepped into the remarkably cool, dark interior of the old house, took in the foot-thick walls and the hand-carved furniture, and Raul brought forth a small wooden keg, its metal braces green with antiquity.

"Have you ever tasted hundred-year-old tequila?"

Burt and Jerry didn't know there was any such thing.

"Then I propose a toast to our successful flight and also to my North American friends who so obviously need it."

They raised the sheer, crystal glasses, and the tequila, Burt decided, tasted very much like hundred-year-old brandy, if that is what brandy tastes like when it gets to be a hundred years old. After the fourth glass he was not too sure about anything, except that it had been a very long day.

Raul wakened them the next morning with thick black coffee.

"We will hunt now, while it is cool, and if you don't mind we will have to go in the tractor because of the rain yesterday.

"Please don't make fun of the tractor," he added, "because I think the mechanic loves it more than his wife."

They chugged, coughed, and lurched across the airstrip and onto a narrow trail into the lush jungle foliage still wet with rain. Vines, ferns, and tropical plants closed in behind them in a perpetual twilight in which yellow-headed parrots cackled overhead and a remarkable variety of brilliantly colored birds, butterflies, and insects fluttered through the foliage.

Once a flock of wild turkeys ran to the right of the trail and stood watching, more curious than concerned, and a raccoon-sized coatimundi scurried across in front of them.

The driver, in badly broken English, had begun to talk of El Tractor.

"We have had him only eighteen years," he smiled, proudly, "but I think he had already two years when we got him. He is the oldest tractor in Tamaulipas, but very strong. Only two piston, but they go sideways, not up and down, very strong."

Jerry was gagging from El Tractor's belching, bluish smoke and remarked that he didn't know John Deere ever built a diesel tractor.

"Oh, he is not a real diesel," the mechanic said seriously, "but he can eat diesel. Since he get so old he can eat anything, gasoline, kerosene, diesel. Today he is eating diesel because there is no gas."

The trail turned out of the darkness of jungle and skirted a succession of small clearings, each red with ripening maize, and swarming with bird life. Bluerock pigeons exploded from the grain and came whistling low over the trees, their red bills distinct in the sun, crossing flights with mourning doves, Inca doves, whitewings, and an occasional string of brownish tree ducks hovering low over the grain.

"My God," said Burt, "what are we waiting for? This is a regular rookery!"

"Yes," smiled Raul, "but first I want you to really see some whitewings."

They passed a cluster of grass-thatched huts, obviously homes of the ranch workers, and naked children tottered out to watch the passing tractor. Then they cleared a small hill, and below was a large natural lake, the water barely visible for the   0209 clouds of whitewings hovering over it like swirling snow, trying to find landing room for a drink. The drying black mud of the shoreline, the trees around the lake, and the hillside beyond were all one swarming mass of whitewing doves.

Raul led them on foot into the low brush, the ground white as if with snow, and Jerry realized that the whiteness was the broken shells of tens of thousands of whitewing eggs.

"Here is the home of many of the whitewings you once hunted in Texas," Raul said proudly. "Once there were hundreds of miles of this brush, but now the clearing has started, and before long it will be gone."

The air was alive with the cooing, rustling, buzzing din of tens of thousands of birds, sounding more like the drone of some giant beehive.

"They are becoming more crowded every year, and they

are changing their flights," Raul explained. "They do not have to go to your country so much for grain because they now have it here. But there will always be enough for hunting if their breeding brush can be preserved in time. Unfortunately," he added, "your country seems to spend too much money to control the gun and not enough to give the birds a place to rear their young. It is the same with your ducks, no?"

"Do you have any of this land for sale?" Jerry asked.

"I think it could be arranged," Raul pondered. "In fact, the two gentlemen you met from Philadelphia are handling some of my interests and perhaps an arrangement could be worked out with them. They will be in McAllen for a few days more."

They got back on the tractor and went to the grainfield, because Raul never disturbed the birds at their watering place, and in the heat of the shooting at bluerocks, whitewings, and the strange brown *Pa Chee Chee* ducks, Burt figured it out.

"You ever stop to think that a couple of gringos have been set up like sitting ducks?" he grinned. "This guy knew you were on the International Wildlife Committee to buy whitewing breeding area; he had you spotted, even had his bankers waiting. You beginning to feel a little like a Yankee in Boys' Town?"

Jerry smiled, making a difficult going-away overhead shot on a big, swift-flying pigeon. "Yes," he said, "I knew. But what our Mexican friend may not know is that we've sent people all over this country to find the breeding area of this particular colony of whitewings. We'd have come looking for him if he hadn't found us; and that way, his asking figure would have come a lot higher.

"So just keep your mouth shut, Yankee," he added, scrambling for more shells. "The way I figure it, we've got at least two more days of hunting and that hundred-year-old tequila left if we can just hang around and haggle a little over prices, Mexican-style."

El Papa Sabalo

The shadow of the Cessna darted across the light sand of the beach where a small river pass entered the Gulf, and Eddie the pilot cocked her up on one wing in a steep, banking climb. Bob Sawyer had seen them too, the dark pod of fish in the lacy white breakers below, looking from that height more like tadpoles in a blue-green pond.

Doyle Brown shut both eyes as the plane came around in a

stomach-sinking sideslip, then straightened up inches above the breakers.

"They're tarpon," Billy Harris yelled. "The surf's alive with them. We can go back to La Pesca and get the boats and be back down here in a couple of hours with the surf this calm."

"Won't be time for that if you want to see the real show," Eddie said, pointing down into the Gulf where half a dozen large, dark shadows rippled the surface. "When those big schools of menhaden hit the surf, it'll be somethin' you boys may never see again. And it won't be long coming."

He banked the plane again low over the green Mexican jungle and made a low run down the beach, checking for wash-outs.

"Tide's low enough we can land on hard sand if you guys are game. There's a village just up this little river if we should crack a landing gear or anything; I expect they've got boats big enough to get us back to La Pesca."

"What you say, old man?" Billy asked Doyle.

"I say my butt is already chewing paperdolls out of this seat, and the next time ole Doyle goes fishing it'll be by train."

Eddie chuckled to himself, made a sharp bank, and came back upwind, pancaking in so perfectly they barely felt the over-sized beach wheels touch down, and then they were bumping and bouncing to a stop beside the water.

Billy shook his head in admiration, wondering how the devil he'd been able to hire a bush pilot with Eddie's reputation for four hundred a month.

They quickly put together the rods and walked the few feet over to the crashing breakers where a great flock of gulls were gathering low over the green swells. From every direction more birds were coming like vultures to an impending massacre.

A school of tarpon rolled in the breakers, a bronze-backed old warrior in the lead which Sawyer figured would go over six feet.

"They're going someplace in a hurry," he yelled to Doyle. "Let's go on around the pass."

The breakers had begun exploding with flying, skittering

bait fish, and the birds were diving and screaming, dipping cautiously to the surface between blasts and coming up with wriggling silver menhaden.

A school of bluefish went chopping into one of the dark shadows of menhaden and the little fish erupted into mercurial drops of silver skittering the surface. Sawyer saw a big blue come clear of the water and throw a silvery object clear, then saw Doyle's rod lurch again with a second strike.

"They're playing basketball with my spoon," he yelled above the noise of the surf and screaming gulls. "Throw in over here."

Snook, bluefish, jacks and tarpon slashed up through the schools of purplish-backed pogies like schoolboys shouldering through showers of jellybeans, butting, slashing and gorging with the birds hovering overhead and big, chug-headed gafftop swirling around them, picking up the cripples.

Lean torpedo shapes of sharks cruised purposefully through the melee, and a small tarpon rolled directly in front of Sawyer, blasted into the menhaden, and then swirled away in terror from a long black fin behind him. The water opened in a thrashing concussion of spray and a dark circle of bloody froth rolled up in the next wave.

Sawyer saw a hulking bulk in a wave, realized it was a tarpon, and threw the plug three feet ahead, reeling fast to pull it past his nose like a panicked mullet. There was a flash, a mighty boil of the water, and a tormented old man of the sea came twisting up as if in slow motion, huge red gills flaring, staring sidewise for an instant at his picadors before crashing back into a breaking wave. Sawyer could not believe his eyes. No tarpon could be that big.

Twenty-pound line was melting from the reel, as the great fish moved ponderously toward the pass. Sawyer tightened the drag, helping the reel with his thumb and running down the beach to save line.

One of the natives who had been watching from the edge of the jungle came racing alongside him yelling *"lancha,"* and Sawyer passed the bucking rod over the heads of Billy and Doyle, who were both fighting big snook.

The little Mexican ran ahead, shoved a dugout canoe off the shoreline of the pass and steadied it as Sawyer stepped in, trying to keep his balance and seeing shiny metal at the bottom of the reel spool.

The boy paddled furiously, and for the first time the reel stopped its screeching. The tarpon was boring ahead, moving with the tide into the jungle-rimmed river.

Sawyer looked back and saw Doyle and Billy scrambling on the beach, silvery fish flopping behind them and the water exploding in front.

Then the huge tarpon rolled and the Mexican boy babbled excitedly.

"Es el papa sabalo," he whispered reverently, "the father of all tarpon."

For what seemed like hours, the tarpon sulked deep. The sun was settling over the jungle, insects began their torture, but Sawyer looked back and the Mexican boy was smiling, apparently enjoying the adventure.

Billy came trotting down the side of the river, yelling that it was getting late and they'd have to fly back to La Pesca.

"Go ahead," Sawyer yelled back. "It'll be lighter without me taking off. I'll be right here when you come back in the morning, maybe fighting this same damn fish."

"You're nuts," Billy shouted.

A few minutes later he heard the plane roaring for take-off, its engine laboring until the sound faded out to sea.

The boy put the paddle in his lap, sat back in the dugout, and pantomimed driving a burro cart. *"Vamonos para la casa, sabalo,"* he said playfully, making the motions of whipping the tarpon.

As if to participate in the game, the tarpon streaked to the surface and made his first clean jump out of the water in more than an hour.

"This cat has nine lives," Sawyer mumbled, disheartened because he had thought the fish was too tired to jump any more. Apparently the Mexican boy understood a little English. He looked at Sawyer seriously.

"Nueve vidas?" he asked in awe.

They came slowly around a curve of the stream and Sawyer could smell food cooking and saw thatched huts in the flickering light of cookfires reflecting in the water. The whole village, apparently, had turned out to watch them and shout encouragement.

"Quieres comer?" the boy asked, making the motions of eating.

Sawyer nodded, realizing he was indeed hungry.

The boy yelled something in Spanish and a youngster paddled out to them with an earthen crock filled with soft tortillas, black beans and fish. Sawyer ate it with his fingers, holding the rod with one hand.

The old tarpon kept moving, around the curve of the river and out of sight of the village, and Sawyer wondered where he was headed, thankful at least that he had gone this way rather than out to sea.

The jungle night closed in around them, and a huge orange moon came up through vine-draped trees hanging over the water.

Fish streaked ahead of them on the placid surface, leaving phosphorescent wakes like shooting stars as they panicked from the canoe.

It was beneath a dark, undercut bank, where the river was slow and deep, that the tarpon sounded. This was the place the old patriarch had been fighting so long to reach, his sanctuary. But for the first time, Sawyer realized he could budge the loggish weight by straining the rod, and gradually he began forcing the monster up, a foot at a time, using thumb pressure on the reel and feeling the line stretch and whine like a fiddlestring.

Suddenly the line began slanting up, a glowing torpedo wake streaked up through the black water and exploded the surface into a shower of phosphorescent sparks in the moonlight. Thrashing his head like a wounded buffalo, the great fish hung there half out of water, and Sawyer knew this was it . . . he put on more pressure, pumping and reeling, and the tarpon and the canoe began converging, an inch at a time, the silver shape gleaming nearer and brighter in the moonlight.

Sawyer felt the dugout tremble and realized the boy was standing with his long-handled fish spear poised.

"No," he yelled.

But it was too late. The spear flashed to its mark and the tarpon thrashed crazily, starting to sink. Sawyer felt all strength go out of him and also all chances for a world record.

The boy paddled over quickly and Sawyer realized that instead of mutilating the fish and disqualifying him for a record, the spear had passed through one gill and into the head, no more than a gaff might have done. Suddenly he was yelling and whooping in victory, and the Mexican boy leaped overboard to hold up the monster until they could get Sawyer's belt through his gills. In awe, he looked down upon the huge body glowing silver in the moonlight, and realized it was twice the size of the boy.

That night he slept on the dirt floor of a hut with three Mexicans and two dogs, covered with palm leaves against the evening chill and feeling the fleas crawling over him in the soft earth.

He heard the drone of the plane at daybreak, and met Billy on the beach. Doyle had not come, and he was glad because there would have been no room for the tarpon.

"What're you gonna do with that thing?"

"Take him back to La Pesca to measure him for the world's record."

Billy shrugged and held his nose. But he knew Sawyer's mind was made up, and he wondered himself how big the giant fish really was. All tarpon look big, but this one was at least seven feet, thick and broad, and he remembered that a world record on tarpon had once been set on the Panuco River not many miles down the coast.

They quickly loaded the plane, Eddie complaining that the tide was covering his vital strip of wet take-off sand. Sawyer got in the back seat, and with the help of the Mexican boy, Billy shoved the huge tarpon tail first into the plane, its head wedged between the front seat and the door.

Water was lapping the wheel on the surf side of the plane and the other was bogging in soft sand as Eddie taxied up the beach to gain the wind.

He turned around with one quick maneuver which splashed salt spray into the windshield, gunned the engine to firewall rpm, and released the brakes. They bumped and bogged slowly up the beach, the little plane vibrating but gaining little speed. The pass and the waves loomed ahead.

Suddenly Eddie began coughing, a racking, sobbing, asthmatic seizure that shook the whole plane. Instinctively Billy reached for the flaps. Coughing violently, Eddie pulled her up and the stall button whined. She caught the wind, wallowing drunkenly, losing ground. Sawyer saw the green water coming up, and felt the big beach tires dip into a wave as she lurched downward, dipping wheels from wave to wave. Instantly Billy threw open the door, and Sawyer helped him shove the heavy, slippery carcass forward. And as it slid out into the air, the plane lifted, cleared a wave and began gaining speed.

Eddie was still coughing violently, struggling to gain control of himself and the plane, and it was then that Billy knew exactly why he'd been able to hire the best bush pilot in South America for four hundred a month!

But back in the little village amazed eyes had seen much more, a giant fish making his last leap to freedom from the plane. And to this day the story is told around campfires along the Soto cLa Marina and the San Rafael of the father of all tarpon who still swims in their rivers . . . with eight more lives left to live.

The London Gun

The so-obviously British gentleman with the muttonchop side-
burns was standing militarily beside a white column of antebel-
lum elegance, looking very much as if he, not Harry Winthrop,
had inherited the mansion and the old Spanish land grants to that
general vicinity of South Texas.

Nick Dyer smiled into his mug of cold beer and decided the
limeys are still the world's coolest con men.

Winthrop was standing beside the Englishman, greeting

guests and looking somewhat stooped by comparison, smiling
with satisfaction that the hunting party for this house guest, none
other than Mr. Lawrence Payne of London, had already been
such a success.

The lunch had turned out particularly well, even for corn-
fed steer buried in the ground and cooked slowly, Mexican style,
for two days. And the right people had come.

"Ah think it's just marvelous," Mrs. Winthrop was saying,
but she never got to say what because Jimmy Callahan, who
owned the local sporting goods store, broke in to ask about fine
European shotguns.

"I know the so-called London gun is supposedly the best in
the world, but really, I mean if a guy can't afford to pay four
thousand and wait a couple of years for delivery, what do you
think about some of the top-grade Italian guns, like the Beretta or
the Perazzi? Aren't they very similar in balance and design?"

"Yeah," said Mike Crawford, his best customer, "and far as
that goes, I've heard AYA in Spain can duplicate a Purdey, piece
for piece, and for about a fourth the price. Far as that goes, you
can buy a Japanese copy of a Browning for three hundred bucks
that'll shoot just as far and last about as long as any of us will ever
live."

"Oohhh?" breathed Lawrence Payne.

"That's right," said Crawford, "so what's really the difference with a London gun when it just comes to shooting?"

A Japanese or a Belgian might have been backed to the wall,
Nick thought, but the Englishman stood straighter and taller.

"Aye suppose one of those little Japanese cars, or perhaps a
lover from the Fiji Islands, might be, shall we say, serviceable,"
he smiled condescendingly, "but one would scarcely care to discuss them at length with others."

"Well stated, Mr. Payne," Winthrop smiled. "In a little
while perhaps we'll show them the difference."

Nick drove Mike and Jimmy over to the pasture to be
hunted, and filled them in on the arrangement he'd made with
Winthrop the night before.

"I laid him a case of scotch that you guys can outshoot the knickers off that stuff-shirted limey."

"Dunno so much about that," Jimmy said suspiciously. "He was talking about lock time, whatever that is, and static balance and hammer fall. Hell, we don't know that much about shotguns."

"You know how to kill quail with 'em," Nick grinned, "and that's the bet."

Harry Winthrop kept a kennel of the finest pointers in South Texas, and for the special occasion he'd brought along his professional trainer to handle them. It was Butler Griffin, in fact, and the two young pointers he was grooming for the field trials which seemed to interest the Englishman the most.

"Are they as, uh, staunch as our setters?" Payne questioned, obviously concerned that one of the pups might jump up on his freshly pressed knickers. "They do seem a bit, uh, boisterous."

Butler had trouble keeping a straight face.

"They're right boisterous, for sure," he said, "but right good at findin' birds in cockleburs and cactus. Setter's a fine dog, sir, but not for this country. It's too hot and too rough."

They had put down the dogs to run off a little steam before they went into the hunting pasture, and Butler watched with interest as the Englishman took from Winthrop's car a black, leather-covered wooden case with many decals and travel stickers on it. With precisioned care he released the catches and opened it, and the others gathered around to see. Therein, cradled in red velvet as if lying in state, rested a delicately beautiful double with classic straight-grip English stock, intricate scroll engraving on detachable sidelocks, and two sets of barrels nestled into their fitted compartments. Mr. Lawrence Payne made the most of the moment, joining the action to the barrels carefully and delicately, snapping the slender splinter of a forend into place with one tiny, perfectly meshing click.

"You're not going to shoot a 12-gauge at quail, are you?" Mike blurted.

"Oh, yes," Payne replied, "but you see our upland load for the 12-bore is essentially the same as your 20-bore loading. Perhaps, say by American standards, it could be considered an over-bored 20-gauge."

He held up a fat, short little shell two and one-half inches long. "Our upland guns are chambered for the very light load, and of course they are rather lightweight weapons. Would you like to feel this one, sir?"

Mike accepted the graceful double as carefully as a bachelor taking a baby, felt its incredibly featherlight heft and balance, but realized the stock was so long, and so high, that when he put the gun up it hung under his shirt sleeve and the barrels seemed to be pointing for the sky.

"Man, I'd shoot three feet high with this thing," he grinned.

"Perhaps not," the Englishman said. "You see we believe in a sight picture which reveals a good deal of the barrel. Great aid to pointing out a target at an angle. By regulating the impacts of the barrels, this particular gun was made to shoot quite low, in fact. It could scarcely be used effectively on driven grouse or pheasant, but I suppose it will suffice for your quail over dogs."

"I see," said Nick. "And do you change guns for every different bird?"

The Englishman looked at him coolly. "Almost any gun can be made to perform satisfactorily on any game if the shooter is sufficiently accustomed to it. But under certain conditions it is more comfortable to shoot a gun bored for a particular type of target, and the incoming target such as driven grouse is easiest met with a gun which shoots relatively high, making it unnecessary to blot out the approaching target to establish the necessary lead in front."

Butler had cut himself a chew of tobacco, eyes squinting in amusement. "What happens," he asked, "if a pair of birds jump and one goes straight away and the other comes hookin' back over your head? Be pretty hard to carry two guns for that, wouldn't it?"

The Englishman snapped his heels together, threw the double to his shoulder at an imaginary going-away bird, and then dropped the gun from his shoulder, whirled with knickered legs crossed awkwardly one over each other, and mounted it again.

"That is the manner in which it is done, in driven grouse shooting," he said. "The first shot is taken as the birds approach, and then the turn is made for the second; one in front and one behind."

Butler shook his head, having trouble keeping from laughing, and Nick realized for the first time the Englishman had begun to redden slightly at the temples.

"Sir, I noticed that you took the gun from your shoulder, then remounted it to simulate the second shot. Is that also established procedure?"

"Indeed, and quite necessarily so for smoothness of swing. The tracking of the target, the swing, and the shot are all accomplished in one movement culminated by the shot at the instant the gun butt touches the shoulder. This eliminates the common American fault of stopping the swing. Thus, after one shot is made, the gun butt is dropped slightly to permit the restart of the cycle."

"I'd think a man would have to cycle pretty quick to get on two of those quail in a thicket," Butler observed. "Let's go see if we can find us a few."

The lemon-and-white dog was tearing over the pasture at breakneck speed. He whipped through a patch of cactus, then whirled in midair and came skidding down sidewise, nose and tail taut as if stretched by some invisible wire.

"Aye say," mused the Englishman, visibly impressed. "Devilishly stylish."

"Fair," said Butler.

The black-and-white dog was honoring the point and they walked past him three abreast. The birds obviously were nailed in a patch of brush at the edge of the timber.

Mike was on the left, Jimmy on the right, and the Englishman was coming up straight behind the dog when the covey exploded, the most of the birds going past Jimmy.

He nailed two, missed the third shot, and Mike powdered a sleeper that came up behind him. The Englishman did not fire.

"What were you waiting for?" Harry Winthrop fumed.

"Rather dislike potting another man's bird," Lawrence

Payne said starchily, glancing at Jimmy, who had blasted the lone quail that jumped ahead of the Englishman.

The singles had fanned out into tall grass well away from the woods, and the black-and-white dog was already down.

"Shall we take turn about?" Payne asked. "Or take them as we may?"

"Since there's a bet on, sir, I'd suggest you just fire at will," Nick said quickly.

"Very well."

They walked in on the singles, this time the Englishman dropping back and working his way to the far left, away from the dog. A quail fluttered up out of the grass and there was an instantaneous report as it folded in a shower of feathers two feet from the nose of the dog.

"Sorry about firing so near the animal, old man," Payne apologized to Butler, "but since there is a bet of sorts, you know."

Butler rubbed his eyes and tried to remember when he'd seen a bird hit that hard, that fast.

They were walking over to the lemon dog, which had come down at the edge of a fencerow, when two birds flushed wild behind them. Nick ducked to the ground, heard two loads of shot go over his head, and saw the Englishman standing there in the awkward, cross-legged stance, blowing the smoke out of his barrels.

"Grassed them both, Aye believe," Lawrence Payne said stiffly to Butler. "Afraid Aye failed to center the second bird, if you'd care to send the dogs for him first."

Nick felt his face flushing in the sun as Harry nudged him and laughed in his ear. "You want to press the bet, young man?"

Mike and Jimmy began missing shots they'd normally kill, trying to shoot too quickly, and the Englishman seemed to need only to point his magic double in the general direction and the birds would fall. Once, as a bird towered and banked overhead, a diamondback rattled in a prickly pear patch beside the Englishman's left foot, and he killed the quail and then, calmly, the snake.

"Rotten sound," he observed.

When Butler halted the hunt to let the dogs water and rest in a little creek, Jimmy and Mike sat disgustedly down on the bridge and the Englishman stood looking into the distance, unwilling to risk dirtying the bottom of the knickers on the boards.

"What is your business back in England?" Nick asked.

Lawrence Payne glanced at Harry, received a nod, and smiled broadly for the first time.

"Actually, Aye suppose my title should be stated as vice president, but my principal function with the company is senior shooting instructor at our grounds just outside of London."

"What company?"

"Oohh, thought you knew, Holland and Holland. Make guns, you know."

"Now," said Nick, slumping to the ground against a tree, "I know."

On the way back they passed the ruins of a tenant farmer's shack with a trashpile and an ancient automobile rusting in the grass behind it, and Jimmy walked up beside Payne and fell into step.

"I'm just curious," he said, "but would you mind shooting that gun just one time at that old car door over there? We'd like to see what kind of pattern that thing really throws."

The Englishman drew himself up and glanced at the rusty old Ford. "Oh, Aye suppose so," he said, restraining a smile. "But it does seem something of a shame. Couldn't we perhaps locate a slightly later model, old chap?"

A Game of Gulf Poker

The marine radio in Frank Hilliard's sea skiff crackled with static from lightning and the garbled chatter between shrimpers and party boats somewhere far out in the Gulf. With a bit of luck and a little more rain, he figured he wouldn't be going fishing at all.

He was putting in a set of new distributor points when he felt the pier clump with authority and looked up to see the tall, bespectacled Mr. Leslie, whom he had really hoped never to see.

"Morning, sir," he said, straightening up and smiling.

"What's so good about it?" Mr. Leslie said, scowling at the sky. "Your esteemed employer seemed to feel it might be a bit too rough to go offshore, but I got him straight on that just now on the telephone."

"You did?"

"Certainly I did. Where I come from, this is exactly the sort of day the big muskies go on the feed. Your, what do you call them, kingfish are something on the order of a muskie, aren't they?"

"Oh yes," Frank said politely, "they both have teeth."

If Mr. Leslie caught the sarcasm, he failed to show it.

"Well, what are we waiting for?"

"Let me get this distributor back in, and then I'll have to call the office," Frank lied. "Couple of things I need to tell the boss before we go."

What he felt like telling the boss was to take it and jam it. Nobody told him when to go into the Gulf. He'd been on it all his life, and he respected it.

J.B. was not at his desk, the secretary said, but he had left a message.

"Take the old boy out the jetties, and give him a good shaking up anyway," the soft voice purred. "J.B. says he's bound and determined to go fishing, and he's the biggest account we've got in Wisconsin."

When he got back to the boat Leslie was sitting in the fighting chair, ready to go.

"I've been listening to the radio," he said, "and they must be playing poker out there. Some captain came on the air and said he had found a pair, picked up a couple of kings, and a jack. What was he talking about?"

Frank winced; he'd probably heard Art Murray on the *Miss Gulf Coast*, or maybe Jack Johnson on the *Williwaw* . . . they were just hardnosed enough to be out fishing in such weather. Which would shoot down any arguments he might have given about it being too bad offshore.

"They're fishing the shrimp fleet anchored about twenty

miles out," he answered, snapping the distributor cap in place and sniffing the bilge for gas fumes. "A pair means the skipper has found a pair of boats anchored one behind the other; the kings are kingfish, the jacks are jack crevalle.

"There's some extra foul weather gear up forward," he added, firing the engines.

"No thanks, I don't expect I'll melt; feels good. This devilish hot and clammy climate you have down here is enough to choke a man. Where I come from," he added significantly, "a person feels a little more like getting out and doing things. Are the fish down here as, uh, desultorily inclined as the people?"

Leslie was standing up beside him as they neared the jetties, looking apprehensively between the rocks at the ugly, rolling whitecaps churning across the bar. Frank figured the trip would be all over after the first three or four big swells. He goosed each engine up to about 2700 rpm, faster than he'd normally hit such seas, and the old boat wallowed into the first one, slid over it in a shower of spray, and half-broached in the trough before he righted her to crash head-on into the next.

For the first six or eight swells, always the roughest crossing the Freeport bar, he was too busy to look at Leslie, but when he did his hopes fell. The man was smiling, holding on and balancing against the pounds and jars, water dripping from his glasses and nose.

"Hey," he said, "that's a bit of sport we don't have back home; hardly ever get that kind of roll to the seas even on the big lakes. Fine boat you have here, Captain. You'd probably enjoy coming up to Wisconsin someday," he added. "If you ever hooked up with just one good muskie, you might not ever want to come home again. Great fish, the muskie, greatest fighter pound for pound in the world."

"How can you say that for sure until you've fought a few of our kingfish or dolphin?"

"Well," Leslie pondered, "there have been hundreds of books and articles written of the muskie's fight and courage, and I don't recall seeing much about your kingfish or dolphin. In fact, I was under the impression that the dolphin was not a sport fish at all, but something of a friend of man. Why would you want to hook one of those?"

Frank groaned inwardly. He'd explained that to every woman, child, and landlubber on the boat for fifteen years.

"The dolphin you're thinking about is a mammal, the one you see on television. I just simplify it by calling the mammal a 'Flipper,' and the dolphin fish a dolphin. The correct word around here for the dolphin mammal is 'porpoise.' "

"Oh, I see," said Leslie.

Frank asked him to hold the wheel on a heading of 155, went back and took the plastic bag of frozen trash fish out of the icebox, and put it into the live well to thaw out faster. Then he took the Penn reels on the heavy boat rods out of the rod holders and put them forward into the cuddy cabin, emerging with two lightweight rods carrying Ambassadeur 5000 reels loaded with fifteen-pound monofilament.

"Since you're a freshwater man," he explained, "thought we'd just use the light stuff today. Tends to make the fish a little more active. Isn't this about the same equipment you'd use on your muskies back home?"

"Matter of fact," Leslie said, "it's almost exactly the same, although I prefer a single-handed rod, a bit more sporting I'd think."

Frank glanced at the horizon, saw something, and looked back again, using the sailor's trick of the corner of the eye. Then he made them out, tiny dots disappearing and reappearing in the swells.

"Shrimpers up ahead," he said, "and I believe they're anchored. When they trawl bottom all night for shrimp, they also catch tons of little fish. At dawn, when they finish the last drag and anchor up to sleep, they throw over the trash fish in cleaning out the nets. The game fish know what's coming. So they just hang around the boats, waiting for the next free meal. The longer a boat is anchored, the more fish are likely to be congregated around and under it. Ling and dolphin hang around under any floating object just for shade, anyway."

"I wouldn't think they'd need much shade today," Leslie said, wiping the rain off his glasses. "And it does seem a bit of a shame your fish have to be scavengers instead of game species such as the muskie or smallmouth bass. No self-respecting muskie would as much as touch a dead fish; he's a killer, you know, a real game fish."

Frank went on thawing the chum, thinking of the times he'd seen kingfish come twenty feet clear of the water feeding upon lightning-fast pilchard minnows. He expected that a muskie would never know which way a pilchard minnow went.

"The idea of all this dead fish," he was saying to Leslie, "is that we start throwing it on the water. It's called chumming. We have to con them into believing it's just another free meal from the shrimper."

"Do you think they might hit one of my muskie plugs?" Leslie pondered, opening his tacklebox and producing a cigar-shaped plastic plug with spinners fore and aft. "I've got a lot of confidence in this little killer."

"Sure, I think they'll take it," Frank grinned. "For keeps."

When the boat swung past the shrimper's stern, Frank threw out a seabucket full of chum, and instantly saw the long, lean shapes darting far below in the blue-green depths. He reversed both engines, backed up even with the shrimper, and killed them, letting the current pull them slowly past her stern, where the surface was already boiling with feeding kings.

The sun had broken out of the clouds and Frank could see the plug hit the water, the whirling spinners flashing silver, then it disappeared in a swirling geyser of spray and Leslie's light rod was whipping like a reed in the wind.

Suddenly the rod straightened and the plug came sailing halfway back to the boat, or at least half of it did.

"Wow," said Leslie, examining the mangled mess of plastic. "It appears whatever that was simply bit the thing in half. What was it, a shark?"

"Nope," said Frank. "Small kingfish."

Leslie tied on the solid wooden floater-diver which Frank recommended, an old yellow-and-black-striped Creek Chub with a metal lip to make it wiggle on the retrieve. But Leslie got to see only one wiggle. A three-foot streak of silver came clear of a wave, the bright-yellow plug securely crunched in its jaws.

"Oops," grunted Leslie, fighting the bucking rod. "I thought you told me kingfish didn't jump like muskies!"

"They don't," Frank said. "A muskie jumps after he's been hooked, or so I'm told. A king doesn't jump on purpose, he's just going so fast when he strikes he can't stop."

Frank watched and waited for the line to break, but Leslie was working the kingfish artfully, never letting him rest, pumping and winding perfectly, and the whipped fish came to gaff.

Just as he started to lift the king from the water, Frank saw a flash of brilliant blue and green whip past the stern, and yelled for Leslie to grab the other rod.

"Dolphin," he yelled. "Get something in the water; all we gotta do is get one on, and the whole school will stay up with him!"

Leslie grabbed the other rod, quickly whipped out a cast with a brightly colored floating plug, and as it touched the water a beautiful golden streak hurtled through the air from three feet to the side and came crashing down on the lure like a cat upon a mouse. Instantly the dolphin was clear again, bouncing the surface, catapulting, twisting, leap after leap successively farther from the boat, the little reel screaming.

Leslie was beaming from ear to ear, rod high and perfectly arched. "There are others all around him," he said, "rather a school of them it seems."

For the next hour they fought and whipped dolphin in an aerial circus during which Leslie's plug was once thrown clear by a particularly wild dolphin, a kingfish hit it in midair, missing the hooks, and before he could reel in another dolphin had streaked off with the plug.

"Are they active enough for you?" Frank grunted, putting pressure on a twelve-pound bull which felt more like forty.

"Fairly so," said Leslie, artfully leading his whipped fish alongside, groping for the gaff without asking Frank's help, and with one smooth movement flipping the bloody, flopping fish into the open icebox.

Suddenly, Frank knew he had been taken.

"You didn't learn that," he said, "in Wisconsin."

Whereupon Leslie began to chuckle, casting at the same time.

"Oh no," he said, "as a matter of fact, I grew up in Florida. But I did learn one thing up in Wisconsin since, and that is that you Texans will, as you say, bust a gut to put a Yankee down. I just figured a little muskie talk might inspire you to find me some fish."

He was still chuckling, Frank not yet sure of how to take it, when they cruised into the marina.

Art Murray and Jack Johnson were sitting upstairs at the Skipper Club and were surprised Frank had gotten into so many big dolphin so close inshore.

"Oh yes," Leslie said, "and they were fairly active specimens, too, particularly on muskie tackle. But I'd be willing to wager I could catch almost as many of them as we did today on a flyrod."

Art leaned back in his chair, ready to reach for his billfold, but Frank raised his hand and shook his head.

"Don't make any bets with this guy," he growled.

"Come now," said Leslie, obviously enjoying the tinkling highball, "and just when I was getting started, shall we say, chumming for you all."

The Price of a Pintail

They had crawled into the sunken plywood blind by the ricefield pond in the predawn darkness, and as the sun climbed the stair stepping clouds of a norther on the horizon the young Labrador and the old hunter were craning their necks at the sky, whining in their respective ways.

"We're out of the flight, boy," Joe said anxiously to Don Gainer. "Look yonder, and yonder."

Pageants of pintails formed undulating patterns of dark lace against the clouds, all well to the north of the blind.

"Can't help it," Don repeated for the tenth time since daybreak. "This is our lease, Joe, and it isn't like it used to be up on Caddo. You can't just move over and get in somebody else's blind."

Two ducks came in from behind, saw the decoys and banked sharply, and Don realized the old man was finally losing his sight. He'd never seen them, which was just as well because it would have been embarrassing for the old-timer to kill a spoonbill.

And kill them he would have; Joe Haynes was a legend with a shotgun. It was said no man could beat him on ducks, and he'd proved it with bets against the best market shooters on the pinoak flats of Arkansas and East Texas in the days when bag limits and game wardens were less bothersome.

"What's that they were telling on you up on Caddo a few years after I left?" Don asked, hoping to change the subject from the pintails. "Something about you nearly freezing to death?"

"Aw," said Joe, "they was stretchin' it. Me an' Bub Marshall was over by Little Green Brake in one of them big boat blinds an' it come a whitecappin' norther, so rough the boat swamped an' sunk right in under the blind. The ducks was flyin' so good we never even noticed until it started gettin' dark."

A flight of teal whipped low over the decoys, but Don knew the old man wouldn't shoot. Little ducks had always been "fuzzy ducks" to Joe Haynes, below his market hunter's dignity.

"We got a little cold with the wind so strong," Joe was saying, "but they found us about an hour before dark the next day an' we wasn't even really what you'd call bad hungry yet."

"What's this about you getting ornery with your rescuers after being missing for thirty hours?"

"Aw, all I said was that I was much obliged they'd come to git us, but since we was already there, an' them mallards was just beginning to fly, how come we couldn't go on an' hunt another hour or so before dark. One of them sheriff's deputies got plumb bilious about it."

The geese began flying, a whooping, honking parade of snows, blues and Canadas across the sky, and the Lab whined and shuddered watching them. Joe took a small nip from the silver flask he'd carried for forty years.

"Damn brant," he said, listening to the derisive yelling high out of range. "Looks like if a man don't care about shootin' at them or fuzzy ducks, the law would let him kill an extra two or three good ducks a day."

A good duck to Joe was a mallard, but because most of his hunting had been in Arkansas and East Texas, the best duck of all was a pintail. They'd brought six bits apiece when mallards were selling for fifty cents a pair. They were scarce in his country, smart and difficult to decoy.

"You remember when you was a little shaver an' me an' your daddy went back in behind Eagle's Nest in the pinoak slash when the bayou was floodin' an' you killed your first greenhead right there standin' by the boat?"

Don remembered. It was one of the reasons he was taking the old man hunting now. He owed some debts which could be repaid no other way, and he hoped the old devil would get started reminiscing about the old days. He'd market-hunted over live decoys for years, before and after the law banned them. Someday there would be no such stories to hear; Joe was the last of a breed.

"You got any English Callers left up on Caddo?"

"Naw," Joe spat disgustedly, "warden sneaked in on me an' Bub a few years back, an' we never seen him until Bub had turned loose that little hen he called Prissy. Now that was a Judas duck! She'd take off after a flight of them wild mallards an' get right in amongst 'em, callin' her head off, an' when she'd come circlin' back to the blind with them wild drakes strung out behind her, I'll swear she'd hit the water paddlin' for the blind to git outa the way of the shootin'."

"So what happened?"

"Well, Bub coulda killed her right then an' the warden would've had hell provin' she was tame. Rest of our decoys was legal, an' she didn't have no band on. But Bub couldn't stand to shoot her, an' when she came flappin' right up into the blind with us, there warn't much doubt about her bein' a live decoy. Cost ole Bub his huntin' license for a year, an' that's likely what give him that stroke he had."

Don waded out and rearranged the decoys for the northerly shift of the wind he could see coming, and hoped Joe's aging eyes couldn't make out the flights of pintails working just across the fence on the next lease. Joe would rather poach a duck than kill one legally.

"What ever happened to that man from Kansas City you used to shoot against all the time, the one that lost so much money to you his heirs were still paying it off when I left East Texas?"

"They never took care of it all, son," Joe said, scanning the sky. "An' there was a lot of tales told about that which wasn't so. They was sayin' up around Stuttgart that I had me a special gun that would shoot ten times without loadin', an' that's how I beat him."

"Well, did you?"

"Naw, it wouldn't shoot but eight times, an' that's countin' one in the chamber. I just made me a magazine extension that went on out nearly to the end of the barrel. Hardly ever used it because it was slow to swing loaded, an' the magazine spring had to be so strong I'd skin up my fingers loadin' it every time I'd get in a rush."

"Wasn't that the guy you beat with the great mirror shot?"

"Wasn't no mirror to it. He'd left his eyeglasses an' tried to back out on the bet. I told him, all right, I'd hunt blindfolded till he caught up with me. But I could see a little out the bottom of the blindfold, an' the water was slick-calm like a mirror. I'd just peep down at the water an' when I seen the shape of ducks reflectin' I'd kinda shoot up where I thought they'd be, an' dammed if I didn't kill two on the first shot."

One thing the old man had not forgotten, Don decided, was how to improve his stories a bit from year to year.

It was shortly after nine when the first really big flights of pintails began coming in from the ricefields on the coast, and

Don watched them in the distance, working low over the prairie and beginning to bank up on a small open pond of ricewater in the stubble.

Joe had seen them, too.

"Now by cracky them ducks is on this same place, because I can see the fence over beyond them," he argued. "What's to keep us from pickin' up a few blocks an' just easin' over there an' settin' up for 'em?"

Don had been afraid he'd ask that. The old man was too weak to walk a boggy, flooded ricefield. And the tragic part was that he wouldn't admit it even to himself.

"Joe, I'll tell you what. There's a board road over there about a quarter-mile where there was an oilwell drilled last year. I'll walk over there, and if it's good enough walking I'll motion for you."

"Oh no you won't," the old man said defiantly. "Jest like your dad, ain't you? Time I get there you'll have them pintails all shook outa there. If you kin walk it, I kin walk it."

They started off with Joe and the Lab in front, Don purposely taking it slow and easy. They found a contour levee which was better walking than the muddy ricefield, and followed it until it turned. Then they cut across, with Joe wheezing and coughing but his eyes locked on the ducks working low over the far end of the field.

Jacksnipe began flushing ahead of them, darting up erratically in twisting, split-second takeoffs that startled the Lab. The dog ran over to where the first pair jumped, smelled the spot with tail wagging, looked at the sky and then back at Joe.

"He's wondering how come you didn't shoot that snipe, Joe," Don needled, hoping the old man would stop and take a breath to talk. "What's the matter, you didn't like the odds?"

"You know very well why I didn't shoot," Joe wheezed. "I'm not about to spook them pintails till we get set up for 'em. An' a jacksnipe ain't all that hard to hit anyway, son. Hell, I've bet on them, too. Used to be a lot of 'em, an' woodcock, an' plover, too. You never got to hunt plover, did you, son?"

"You changed the subject from jacksnipe," Don said, stopping to rest. "Far as I can see they're about the toughest target in shotgun shooting."

"True," said the old man, "if you shoot at the wrong time. Now you watch the next one that gets up. He'll make one big dart to one side or another an' that's the time to shoot if you're quick. If you ain't, then wait. He'll nearly always chirp an' then crap, an' right after he craps, he'll straighten out an' you can kill him then."

"What if he's constipated?"

"No use tryin' to help this younger generation," the old man wheezed, still walking.

The pintails were beginning to get up ahead of them, well out of range, milling uncertainly. And when they reached the oil-well road, the air was full of ducks, circling and trying to come

back into the little low spot in the stubble which had been filled with fresh water by rain.

"Now there is the gentleman of ducks," Joe said, watching them cup wings and glide. "Allus wears his tux an' his gray checkered vest, allus looks clean an' white, like he jest got his suit out of the cleaners."

Some of the ducks were getting up within range, and Joe was picking up speed with solid footing beneath him. His eyes were on the little flat pond, the white feathers drifted by the wind against the stubble, and the muddied water where the ducks had been feeding and preening. He was sizing up the layout for a makeshift blind and the decoys.

Suddenly he stopped, and Don knew instantly that his worst fears were realized. The old man's face was gray, sweat popped out on his forehead, and unsteadily he leaned on his gun and sat down on the board road, holding his chest.

"Joe, are you having another heart attack?"

"Naw," he lied, looking up like a small boy caught in the pantry.

"Now listen, Joe, if you want to die duck hunting, that's fine. But you're not gonna do it with me. You sit right there, or lie down on the boards here and rest. I'm going to get the Jeep."

"Dammit, son, a man has the right to die where he damned well pleases. Look yonder!"

The first flight of pintails had returned, flying low against the wind and looking suspiciously at the pond.

"Let me have your shell bag," Don snapped, "and your gun."

He grabbed the old automatic and fired it three times into the ground to empty it, threw the shell sack as far as he could out into the stubble, and began running down the board road.

It was a long way, and he was barely halfway back in the Jeep when he heard the ominous single shot. So that was it, the old man had somehow hidden one last shell, a sort of viking's funeral for an old duck hunter. Don shuddered, and cursed himself, realizing that was exactly the way the old man would want to go and thinking what that full-choked old gun could do to a man's head.

He drove as fast as the Jeep would stay on the ground, turned onto the board road, and with a quick flood of relief saw the old man still sitting there, hunched over, but with his duck caller on his lips.

Six pintail drakes had cupped wings and were heading straight for him, and when they suddenly flared to climb, the lead pair dropped simultaneously with a single shot.

The Jeep skidded to a stop, and the old man had slumped forward again, his head on his chest. But when Don got his arms under him, the aging body was able to help a little, and he saw a victorious smile on the weathered face, which was beginning to regain its color again.

"You crazy old fool, you could have killed yourself."

"Son, you don't understand. Them was pintails, all drakes, too, an' the lead pair crossed jest right for a double."

By the time they got to the highway, the old man was sitting up feeling for his flask, which Don had also taken from him along with the shell bag.

"Tell me one thing," Don asked. "I emptied that gun and threw away the shells. Where'd you get those last two rounds?"

"Get 'em?" the old man smiled weakly. "Now you never thought ole Joe Haynes would be huntin' with a plugged gun, did you, son?"

Two Boys

The norther had passed in the night, spewing rain and thrashing limbs against the roof, and the morning sky was a cold, metallic blue, as if the swirling clouds had scoured summer from the sky.

Dead leaves chased the wind across Wallisville Road, pelting the small figure walking briskly beside the road and carrying a shotgun as if he had very important things to do.

I stopped and backed up and he came running, a comedy in

cut-down camouflage parka with sandy hair, freckles, and big, in-quisitive blue eyes which looked strangely familiar.

"Aren't you Sam Buckner's boy?"

"Yessir, sure am. Billy Buckner."

"Didn't know he had a boy big as you. Where you going to hunt?"

He looked back at the back end of the pickup, appraising the piles of clothing, hip boots, and cased shotguns.

"Well, sir, I'd thought about just walking off down toward the marsh and doin' best I could. Me and daddy was supposed to go today, but he had to pull a sick man's shift over at the plant. He don't let me run the boat by myself yet, so I'll just see if I can pass-shoot me a few teal and blackies along the shoreline. Where you gonna hunt?"

I told him the areas as we rode toward the marsh, and he brightened immediately. "That's up by Jack's pocket, over on the other side of the river. Yeah, we went over there a couple of times last year; lots of ducks."

I could see his mind working fast, because we were nearing the big bridge over the Trinity River where he'd have to stop if he was going to walk-hunt the shoreline.

"I guess I shouldn't ask," he blurted, "but if you'd like some company, I'm a good hand with decoys and I can handle a boat."

I'd been wanting to ask him to go, but we had to drive back to a pay phone first; it's a big responsibility taking a boy out into a big marsh with a norther blowing. And it wasn't really a very good trip, anyway, since I only planned to brush the blind and get out decoys for the next day.

"Thanks for offering to take him," Sam yelled into the phone above the refinery clamor. "That kid would rather hunt and fish than eat, and I'd as soon he was doin' that as standin' around on the streets."

So we rode back toward the marsh, and Billy filled me in on the local situation. "Lots of squirrels this year," he informed seri-ously, "and more big trout than I've seen in a long time. We could sure catch us a bunch of fish today if we had time."

I asked how he knew these things.

"By the signs," he confided. "You notice how the syca-mores are just about through turning now, more brown leaves than red ones? Well, that's one sign. My dad says the trees know when to shed same as the shrimp know when to leave shallow water. And because the shrimp go down in the mud is why the trout get so hungry.

"Out there in the bay all you have to do is ride around and watch those old gulls and when you see a bunch hovering or maybe some just sittin' on the water you get over there and chunk a spoon or a red-and-yellow Mirrolure over in under 'em and let it go right to bottom. Those big old yellowmouth specks will try to take it away from you."

By the time the old outboard cleared her throat and warmed up, we were moving out into the slow current of the Trinity, heading south into the half-land, half-water vastness where the river spills over into marsh cane and muck at the end of her jour-ney through the heart of Texas.

For centuries, waterfowl have funneled every fall into these ancestral wintering grounds of brackish bayous and grassy is-lands, shallow water and the silt of centuries oozing sulphurous smells of decaying vegetation with every step by man or beast, where the birds know they are safe.

Although the imported nuisance of the nutria has cut down most of the taller cane, and a few oilwell structures jut above the horizon, the old marsh at the end of the Trinity is probably much the same drab, brown vastness as when the cannibalistic Caran-cahua Indians watched for game and enemies from the high tim-bered bluffs of the shoreline.

We turned into a deep-cut bayou, and wound through patches of head-high cane into the entrance of a smaller tidal in-let, then got out and pulled the boat over the shallow spot I knew was there but always hit anyway.

The blind was a gaunt skeleton with most of the brush gone, so weathered it looked a part of the marsh. I used the machete to cut a load of cane, and we quickly worked it into the rusted chicken wire around the framework. With two hours of daylight left, the last decoy was bobbing in the shallow water.

Teal, widgeon, and gadwalls had been buzzing us while we worked, and snow and blue geese high in the blue sky had never stopped their clamor. I'd watched the boy's eyes follow them, but he never said a word about hunting until he caught a low string of dots across the marsh.

"Boy, look at that," he groaned, "those black mallards ought to fly just before sundown, and boy would I like to get a crack at them."

It would have been criminal not to at least give him a chance, so we hid the boat and climbed into the blind, and I noticed he carried the rust-pocked old 20-gauge Remington automatic the right way, safely and with one hand over the open action to keep the salt spray out. Sam had trained his boy well.

"It'll be my first chance at a black mallard in a long time," he was saying excitedly, eyes roving the sky. "Over where we hunt we get a good many pintails and teal, but it's a little bit open for mallards. They like this tall cane, and ain't much left of it in this marsh."

His fixation for the blacks fascinated me, possibly because the Texas mottled duck has always been my own king among ducks, the smartest, wisest of them all . . . too smart to fly all the way back to Canada and rear his young, he does it in his native marsh, along the golden crescent of the Gulf Coast. And he has done a sufficiently good job of protecting his broods from predation and himself from guns that he is one of the few species of ducks on this continent holding his own in population.

A long line of lesser scaup swung in from the open water of the bay, saw the decoys and bunched into a tightly knit knot as they swung back into the wind, hurtling straight at us, head high and hitting sixty.

The boy made no attempt to raise his gun as they passed. "No use makin' a lot of noise over them," he said. "Those black mallards are smart, and those blackies aren't worth pickin' anyway."

It was obvious who did the duck picking around Sam's place.

I blew a few squawks and chuckles to loosen up the reed of the worn old Yentzen caller, and also the mellow, big-barreled Arkansas caller which if properly and softly chuckled can fool a mallard hen at ten paces.

It was then that six old blacks came in from behind, somehow didn't see us nor hear us, but they had heard the call. A hen rasped it out right back from high in the air, and I watched the boy freeze without looking up.

They passed on over, locked wings and whipped back. Suddenly they were there, hovering, feet down. Neither of us moved, and they dropped into the decoys, sat for an instant with heads up, realized the fraud, and the hens screamed the alarm call and went straight up, black wings beating, heads craning. I took the two on my side, held a foot high as they climbed, taking plenty of time because there was no rush and an over-under only shoots twice. I heard his 20-gauge crack three times, a little too rapidly, and when it was over, three blacks were kicking their last in the decoys and the other three were disappearing over the cane.

"Oh pooh!" he stomped the floor of the blind. "I'll never get a chance like that again! Right there on top of us and I get so excited I shoot right at 'em the first two times. That one I killed was on the last shot! But weren't they beautiful, coming in like that, right on top of us!"

By the time I dropped him off at home, it was nearly an hour after dark, and concern wrinkled Mollie Buckner's brow when she opened the door. But it quickly changed to a smile.

"Come in," she offered, "and don't look at this mess of a house. I've been out in the yard trying to make some kind of sense out of those decoys and junk of Sam's; he had to work today, and you know a duck hunter, he just has to be ready to go tomorrow!"

The house was small, with spotless white woodwork and linoleum on the floors, and the furniture had obviously weathered a family and several dogs, one a flop-eared puppy who promptly began trying to untie my boot laces.

"Just shove him out of the way if you can," she smiled. "Billy brings home every living thing he sees, and you know how it is around here. People drop kittens, puppies and whatever else they don't want at that Trinity River bridge and the poor things are usually half starved when he finds them. I'll bet we've had fifty dogs and cats since he got big enough to prowl that riverbottom."

It was nearly ten o'clock when I drove in the driveway and started unloading things. And when a bicycle pulled up beside the curb it startled me.

The boy was maybe thirteen, with the full-beatle haircut and buttondown collar, and he had seen the ducks being taken from the icebox.

"You write for the paper, don't you?"

"That's right."

"You don't look as young as your picture."

"Thanks."

"You ever kill anything dangerous, like lions, or tigers? I

could shoot dumb old ducks like that with my pellet gun." He whipped the powerful, CO-2-powered gun around, pointing it straight at me and made the explosive mouth noises small boys make to duplicate the sounds of gunfire.

I shoved the barrel aside instinctively, and told him never to point it at anybody again.

He didn't seem impressed. "You know any real writers, I mean book writers? How come you don't write something good like James Bond or something? They got some real adventure in those Bond movies, I mean like those neat poison daggers that flip out of their shoes. Wonder what kind of poison they used on those? It only took twelve seconds to kill. Can you buy poison like that at a drugstore?"

"Now what do you need with dagger poison?"

He reached into a pocket and I saw the glimmer of steel and heard the click of a switchblade opening.

"You ever get to go hunting?" I asked him casually, ignoring the knife. "Or is all your adventure on television? You probably couldn't take wading a marsh anyway."

"Big deal, wading a marsh," he said, but his eyes had lightened up considerably. "You tryin' to ask me to go hunting sometime?"

I told him it so happened I would be going the next morning with Sam Buckner and his boy, and that the blind would hold four if he wanted to go . . . also that I'd go with him to get permission, but first to give me the knife.

"Just don't say anything about the pellet gun," he warned. "They don't know I got it yet."

When I rang the doorbell half an hour later, a white-coated doorman answered. The lady of the house was right behind him, cigarette in one hand and glass in the other.

"Where in the world have you been, and who is this man with you at this hour of the night?"

I broke in and told her what had happened, who I was, and that I'd offered to take the boy hunting.

"We don't happen to enjoy the killing of things, Mr. Brister," she said acidly. "Just the other night some mighty hunter found it necessary to kill our old, almost blind cat and leave his body in our yard. Nor do we particularly admire the guns which have created so much sorrow in this world, nor your so-called National Rifle Association which has prevented us from effectively controlling these weapons. Our women's club has fought you and your lobby hard, Mr. Brister, and we're just getting started."

"Aw, Mother, cool it!"

"One more word out of you and you don't get to go to the dance Saturday night!"

"Big deal."

She yanked him inside, the door slammed in my face, and suddenly I knew a lot more about the boy, this country, and an old blind tomcat with a little lead pellet fired straight into his brain by James Bond.

Professor Tequila Joe

Ray Ramstead saw the flock of gulls diving and working the Mexican shoreline of Falcon Reservoir, knew there would be black bass under them, and cursed the stupid girl back at the lodge who had sufficiently mixed up his bookings to provide him with two parties to guide the same day.

On the middle seat of the big aluminum boat, feeling no mortal pain, were two Louisiana gentlemen sipping from a thermos of tequila margaritas and rearing to catch some bass and then head for Boys' Town.

At the bow in pith helmet and khakis, demanding that his reservation be honored to the fullest, was Professor Joseph Critchell Watlington, who was determined to take back to Harvard with him proof that the flooded city of Old Guerrero had been built on mounds concealing a much earlier civilization.

Ray had at least made it almost to the old city before the bass showed, and he nosed the boat quickly into the shoreline and bailed out with his rod and reel.

"I'm sorry, professor," he yelled, "you'll just have to walk from here. We'll pick you up about noon."

The Louisiana men were already wading out through the murky shallow water to the ledge where the gulls were working.

The professor watched curiously, wondering if sport fishing is not some powerful prehistoric impulse remaining in modern men who no longer need to catch fish to live. He watched them lean forward, as if stalking some game creature, casting as if their lives depended upon it and reeling excitedly when small bass attacked their surface lures. He took out his notebook, scribbled a few words to remind himself to pursue this fishing theory further, and walked up the shoreline toward the flooded city.

Knee deep in the tepid water, Boudreau LaBoeve watched the slight, almost mincing figure disappear in the brush along the shore.

"Now ain't he something?"

"But what?" asked René Thibodeaux, stringing a two-pound bass which had mistaken a white Chuggar for a shad. "Look to me like he de kinda sissy dat got to step outa de shower to pee."

The water erupted with fleeing shad and striking bass, and they both got strikes almost as the plugs hit the water. Ray had a bigger one on a spoon which he was letting settle down below the action where the big bass wait for cripples.

The professor had timed his visit to a period of low water, when irrigation drainage dropped the lake level to reveal most of the flooded city, and he followed a rubble-strewn street where empty windows stared down upon what had been a beautiful plaza beside the Rio Grande.

Seeking shade, he entered a magnificent old church, its floor caked with dried mud, and passed through arched doors into a garden where flowers were blooming in the rich, grass-grown silt. He climbed a low wall, watching for snakes and scorpions, and felt the wind cool and refreshing through the arches of the church.

It was when he opened his knapsack and produced the battered thermos which had weathered so many expeditions that he realized the Cajuns had played the ultimate joke upon a teetotaler. Instead of iced tea, the first swallow choked in his throat like poison and he spat it on the ground. In a deserted city in temperatures of one hundred and ten degrees he was left with no liquid other than a thermos of some miserable mixture of alcohol!

He permitted himself two measured icy swallows and a pungent, tangy taste lingererd in his mouth and nose. He suspected it was some mixture of tequila and lime juice; surely they would not poison him.

As he jotted notes on his core samples, he absently sipped more, feeling a curious tingling glow spread through his body.

He had worked for an hour, attempting to correlate his findings with those of similar cities built over mounds farther into the interior, when he thought he heard voices. He looked up and caught a glimpse of movement in the trees of the churchyard.

A teen-aged Mexican boy stepped into an opening in the bushes, laughing and half-dragging a girl whose flowing hair shone black as a raven's wing in the sunlight. The boy pulled her down to the grass beside him, and as they talked the professor took a long, cool drink from the thermos and suddenly felt very much like God looking down upon the Garden of Eden.

The bushes and flowers were in full blossom, insects buzzed softly, and somewhere across the green mesquite hills a goat bell tinkled in the tranquility of siesta time.

The girl was struggling to avoid the boy's kisses, and he sat up and pouted as if to go. The girl plucked a flower and tickled the back of his neck, and suddenly the boy whirled and threw her to the grass as a young lion weary of play, and the tawny young lioness struggled no more. The professor heard her low moan of pleasure and felt the tequila pounding through his veins. The boy had fumblingly opened her blouse, and instinctively the professor turned his head in modesty. But to move or warn them would spoil their Eden and his.

For the first time in forty years he saw jutting young breasts upthrust and taut, the satiny smoothness of young skin in the sunlight. His pulse pounded in his ears and he drank long and deeply from the thermos, and in his mind's eyes saw again a golden haystack on an Iowa farm and the flowing dark hair and tanned young body which had pulled him down into a much earlier Eden.

Long after the couple left he sat there lost in the past, and when Ray nosed the outboard into a flooded street, he saw the old man walking unsteadily to them as if in a trance.

"Hey, Boudreau, de professor goes for dat Louisiana tea!"

"Yeah," whispered Ray, "and now we've got to take him with us if we go across to Boys' Town. I can't take him back to camp like this."

The cool breeze of the boat's progress, the green water gliding liquidly under the bow, the science-fiction scenery of gaunt, dead huisache and mesquite along the shorelines . . . all was uniquely beautiful to the professor.

He took out his notebook and jotted a reminder to himself to study the type of cactus used in the production of tequila, and whether the plant contains certain hallucinatory or perhaps aphrodisiac properties.

When they passed through the babbling, bustling streets of the border town, the professor savored every smell, every splash of color, and the rows of neon signs and bars with pushcart vendors and beautiful girls in gaily colored dresses on the streets crossed his consciousness like images in a dream.

And then they were in a dark place as cool as a cave, smelling of freshly squeezed lime and the perfume he now recognized as tequila. It was in his nostrils, in his body, and he reveled in the sensation of it.

Everywhere were beautiful girls, young girls. Four came to their table and sat down, and one smiled at him. A waiter in white brought a delicate, long-stemmed glass with salt encrusted around its rim. He tasted the salt, then sipped the mixture, and realized that the two had by some marvelous discovery of the past been mated to attain a perfection of thirsty desire followed by cooling satisfaction.

"Easy now, professor," Ray chuckled. "Ole Margarita can slip up on us gringos."

"Indeed," smiled the professor, trying to remember whatever it was he was going to ask about the hallucinatory properties of cactus, but finding his eyes upon the small, firm breasts of a creature in a yellow dress beside him. He thought of the morning, and the girl in the churchyard, and how she had looked in the sun.

Boudreau punched Ray. "Look at that horny ole devil," he whispered. "You pinch him on the ear right now, he's gonna honk like a French bicycle."

The professor was studying the faces around the table, noting the stamp of races upon them. Ray was the epitome of the Irish, the Louisiana-French was unmistakable in the other two, and the large noses and heavy lips of the Indian influence was clear in the girls. But the one beside him was different. Her nostrils were narrow and aquiline, her features delicate.

Ray noticed his stare. "She's high-grade, professor," he grinned. "They've got all flavors over here, but I expect this one had some Irish ancestors from that old settlement down around Monterrey. Want me to talk to her for you?"

"No," said the professor, "I speak five languages, among them Spanish, and I doubt your assumption as to her lineage. I once did some research near Madrid, and I detect definite Moorish qualities to the chin line."

The professor spoke to her with the slight lisp of Castilian Spanish, and her eyes widened and she smiled.

The others left to dance, and the professor talked with her more, of her sad childhood, her happiness at finding a gentleman so unlike the others. He felt her hand under the table, and she pulled it into her lap, and he felt the incredible smoothness of skin, and a stirring within him which suddenly wiped away fears and years.

The professor and the girl were gone when Ray came back to the table, and he was immediately worried. He had seen the old man flash a fat billfold when he paid for the drinks.

"Don't worry," Boudreau laughed. "He got to be gone a long time, old as he is."

"Yeah," said René, "de worryin' comes later. I know one man from Opelousas dat come down heah to do two things, to kill a jaguar and screw him a Mexican. Ten days later he was wishin' he screwed the tiger an' shot de Mexican."

Evening passed into night in a city within a city, where every night is a fiesta and every street a Mardi Gras of guitars, neon and girls walking the muddy streets with men from around the world.

Ray was shouldering through them frantically, asking street vendors, shoeshine boys, girls he knew. No one had seen a balding old man and the light young girl called Rosita.

It was 4:00 a.m. when a street urchin of a shoeshine boy finally took him to a house, blocks away from the bedlam of Boys' Town, and he knocked on the door with the persistence of desperation.

He recognized the girl immediately and grabbed her before she could shut the door.

"Donde esta el?"

"I'm right up here, young man," he heard the professor. "Come up and taste this magnificent dish she calls *huevos rancheros.*"

Ray took the steps two at a time, suddenly furious at the time and the trouble this old fool had caused him for a twenty-five-dollar guide fee.

"Sit down, my boy," said the professor apologetically. "I am very sorry to have caused you such obvious concern. I shall be happy to pay you whatever you suggest for your trouble."

"Let's go," said Ray, "right now."

The professor sat with his feet propped upon the table, looking out the window.

"All my life," he said deliberately, "I have done the things I should have done . . . attained my degrees, educated my children, buried my wife. And now," he said, "I am going to do what I want to do. Here I have found my Valhalla, my fountain of youth."

"Professor," Ray broke in. "Do you even realize that this young girl, although beautiful, is also a prostitute?"

"Indeed," he smiled. "We have discussed that at length, since it would be rather absurd for either of us to present ourselves as virgin."

He watched the lights twinkling across the city. "Strange customs we have, on both sides of the border. On our side, the simple, biological fact of an old man's attraction for young and beautiful girls is condemned, ostracized and hidden in apartment projects and secretarial bonuses. Over here, this fact is accepted, yet another biological eventuality, a young girl's possibility of becoming pregnant from some childhood lover . . . is condemned much more than in our civilization. This child was thrown out by her family at the age of sixteen, as is the custom here, and is now paying back her indentured bondage in the only way she can . . . to those who kept her and the baby alive in the meanwhile."

Ray stood to leave. "Professor," he said firmly. "The time has come."

The professor rose to his full height, eyes shining defiantly behind horn-rimmed spectacles.

"I am not going back," he said, "ever."

"What on earth do you plan to do over here?"

The professor pulled the girl to him gently, stroking the smoothness of back, waist, and the firm, rounded curve of buttocks and thighs, savoring each meticulously molded part of this planet's most magnificent machine.

"Well, the first thing," he smiled, "Rosie and I are going to try and make up for a great deal of wasted time."

Tiro al Pichon!

In the unaccustomed luxury of the Cadillac's air conditioning, Bob Bernard kept getting the sensation the whole thing was some sort of dream. But the butterflies in his stomach were very real as they drove up the dusty road toward the competition ring.

J. P. Minor stopped at an intersection and asked a couple of Mexican boys standing beside the road for directions.

"*Tiro al pichon, si,*" one of them smiled, pointing to the turnoff. "*Buena suerte!*"

"He wished us good luck," Minor grinned. "They're probably going to the shoot, too. Poor people come for miles to pick up the birds killed in competition, and the rich ones come to see it. The International Championship is one of the biggest events on the border."

Bob was listening, and also looking. He saw a large circle marked off with brightly colored plastic banners, and he saw a live pigeon suddenly clear the horizon, coming up remarkably fast, and go darting and twisting out of the ring.

"Somebody missed one," Minor observed.

The butterflies began doing acrobatics. Where Bob came from in the thickets of East Texas, shooting was at doves jumping wild in goat-weed pastures and quail exploding out of myrtle thickets; any man who couldn't hit a bird the size of a pigeon thrown up in front of him shouldn't be carrying a gun. Visions of winning vast sums of money from idle-rich city folk danced in his head.

"Looks easy, doesn't it?" Minor grunted. "Well, let me tell you right now before we go any farther that this is going to be the most difficult shooting you ever did in your life. It's going to require every bit of timing, reflexes, coordination, and gun pointing savvy you have, plus the ability to perform under pressure."

Bob was confused. "The other day when we were dove hunting, I thought you said I could make us money doing it."

"That's right," said Minor, "I think you can. But there are two promises I want you to make in exchange for the five hundred I plan to invest in that idea. One is that you'll not drink a drop of whiskey the whole shoot, even at night, and that you stay out of Boys' Town."

"Yes, sir. I didn't come down here to find a girl; got one back home I'd like to have the money to marry."

A flock of Mexican boys were gathered around the car, oblivious to the dust swirling up around them as other cars arrived, pecking at the windows and pointing at the car's trunk.

"They want to help us unload," Minor said. "Poor little devils would carry this car into that ring for a quarter."

As they entered the competition ring, Bob felt the butterflies turn into bullbats. He had not realized it would be this big, so many people. The flags of Mexico, Texas, the United States, and the banner of the Mexican gun club fluttered in the hot, dry wind, and the mariachi music, the smell of food cooking over an open fire and the bustling crowd created a sensation of a circus. There was a crackling of excitement in the air, and in the way the crowd watched the small, roped-off square in the center of the big ring.

A short, stocky Mexican stood ready with a live pigeon in his hand. A shooter carrying an obviously expensive side-locked over-under stepped up behind him, within five steps it seemed, and took a great deal of time getting his gun set and mounted to his shoulder.

"I thought they were just practicing," Bob remarked. "Why's he taking it so seriously?"

"Because they're shooting in a miss-and-out, where everybody puts up twenty dollars and whoever stays the longest without a miss wins the pot. I expect there's pretty close to a thousand in this one."

"Can I get in one of those?"

"Not yet. You need to know the rules and watch a while to get the feel of it. See those white lines on the ground," he pointed. "They mark off the thrower's rectangle from the shooter's area. You have a lane twenty yards long and ten wide to do your maneuvering and getting set to shoot. The thrower has exactly the same space in front of you."

"What are those tall posts for, and the rope?"

"For the safety of the *colombaire,* or thrower. A pigeon must clear that rope to be a legal bird. That gets the bird up high enough, at least to start with, to clear the *colombaire* from the line of fire. But plenty of times the bird will dart right down low and the thrower has to hit the ground to get out of the way."

They walked through the crowds and Bob recognized many of the shooters from their pictures in the papers and magazines as some of the top skeet and trap champions in the nation. Many of them had pins and patches on their jackets and hats from shoots all over Texas and Louisiana.

"I had no idea this pigeon shooting was so big, or that people would come from so far to do it," he questioned. "How come we never see any publicity on them back home?"

"That's a good question," Minor pondered. "Maybe the sponsors of the shoots don't want to risk getting tangled up in legalities over the humane laws. There's no law technically against the sport, but I guess they feel it's best to leave well enough alone."

"I can't see how this is any more cruel than any other kind of game shooting," Bob argued. "Here they go out and retrieve every bird, but in field hunting the cripples often get away."

"That isn't the point," Minor said. "We're shooting competition, and not everyone would see why we don't just use clay targets or something. They wouldn't understand that wingshooting is what shotguns are all about, and that the real way to determine wingshooting champions is on live birds."

Bob was still a bit confused.

"In other words, if somebody decided to have a shooting championship like a field trial or at some pheasant or pen-raised quail shooting resort, it would be fine? They could shoot pen-raised birds all day that don't have a chance compared with the odds these pigeons have, but pigeon shooting has to be kept quiet because of what somebody might say or think who doesn't understand it?"

Minor nodded. "And the strangest thing about it is that most of the birds being used here would be dead already if it weren't for the shoots. Birds used in the Texas shoots come from professional trappers, most of them from the Midwest where they're such pests around municipal buildings, grain elevators, and such that the trappers are paid to get rid of them. In some cities they're a serious health problem because they carry diseases, encephalitis in particular. Before the pigeon shoots got popular, most of the birds trapped by professional exterminators went into pet food."

Bob watched another shifting, twisting pigeon go hurtling out of the ring untouched.

"I doubt if one ever got out of a can of cat food," he grinned. "If I were a pigeon, I'd rather take my chances right here."

Someone killed a bird on a long, beautiful crossing shot and the crowd applauded wildly. A Texan in big cowboy boots walked over with a fist full of money and slapped Minor on the back.

"Got three left in the miss-and-out, Lovett, Mallory, and McFaddin. Who do you like for a hundred?"

"Wait till I see how they're shooting," Minor chuckled. "Don't try and catch a mullet cold, Bruce."

Bob watched the three shooters remaining, all making spectacular shots, and twice the *colombaire* hit the ground as a bird dived low in front of him.

"I don't know whether I could shoot right over a man's head like that," he worried.

"You can," Minor said. "Those guys know what they're doing; sometimes they'll move their heads just enough to let you shoot past one ear, the way a bullfighter gambles with a close pass. But they're watching your gun barrel, and if it starts coming too close, they're on the ground in a second."

"They've got to be brave," Bob decided.

"Brave, smart and stronger than you'll believe until you get out there. If somebody told you a man could throw a live pigeon away from you with two shots in your gun, you'd never have believed it, would you?"

"I still don't," Bob said steadily.

A husky bear of a man in a blue shooting sweater stepped out of the crowd and shook hands with Minor.

"Papa, I want you to meet a new shooter, Bob Bernard."

The big man stuck out his hand and smiled. "That's the future of the game, these youngsters," he said, "and if I can help in any way, just let me know. I've shot every shotgun game there is," he added significantly, "and this is the toughest, but the best of them all."

As he walked away, Bob tried to read the patches on his shooting sweater, some of them faded with age. "Captain All-American Skeet Team, Captain All-American Professional Trap Team, T.A.P.A. All-American." He could not read them all before the big man ambled into the crowd.

"You're looking at one of the great ones of all time, boy," Minor said. "If he tells you something, listen."

"You mean I have to shoot against somebody like that?"

"Son, this is one sport in which the pros shoot right along with everybody else. And that's one of the great things about it. Whoever goes out there and wins is, that day, the finest shotgun shooter that day, and it doesn't matter if he's a professional or an East Texas quail hunter."

At ten o'clock the next morning there was a short ceremony, the Mayor of Nuevo Laredo made a short speech, there was a prayer and the playing of the Mexican National Anthem, and the flags went up. Then the music changed to something more on the order of a bullfight's *corrida* and a big cheer went up from the crowd.

Bob saw the two *colombaires*, powerful, graceful men, walking out into the shooting area much like bullfighters entering the ring, and there was more cheering. The International Championship was on!

The first shooter was a lanky young man from Oklahoma,

with All-American trapshooting patches on his jacket, who coolly pulverized two dipping, fast-flying pigeons almost before Bob could see them clear the rope. A lump came into his throat, and now he knew Minor hadn't been stretching a thing.

The judge was calling off names of shooters entered in the main event, and as each shot Bob watched the movements of the *colombaire,* the erratic twisting flight of the birds, and he began to feel a mounting confidence. More were being missed than were being hit, and some of the shooters had obviously been spending more time at the bar than in the ring.

But when he finally heard his name called over the loudspeaker, a strange fear suddenly gripped him. What if he missed? Minor had paid all his expenses. He would look silly. And his gun was a beat-up old Remington automatic. Would they be laughing at him as he walked out?

He fought for composure, walked out into the ring, and put two shells into the automatic. He checked the safety and forced himself to think about the bird and not the thrower.

"Listo?" the Mexican said.

"Pull." As if in slow motion he saw the broad, white shoulders whirl gracefully. A big blue pigeon went up with surprising speed, darted just as he touched the trigger, and in panic Bob realized the bird was getting away, suddenly far out into the ring. Instinct pulled the barrel ahead and as the gun exploded, so did the bird.

"Great second barrel!" somebody in the crowd yelled.

He could scarcely remember the other bird, except that he got him also on the second shot.

Minor was waiting when he stepped off the line.

"Now you see what I mean?" he grinned. "You shot great; everybody gets a little stage fright at first; you'll get over that. Main trouble is that you need a two-barrel gun. You're handicapping yourself with that tight choke on the first shot."

They walked down to the practice ring, where a young thrower was performing, and Bob tried Minor's lightweight, beautifully engraved Browning. He didn't touch either bird.

The big man with the All-American patches on his sweater was sitting on the end of the practice bench, watching with interest.

"You shot over both of them," he smiled. "That gun is probably too high-stocked for you. Feel this one."

Bob thanked him and pointed the old man's automatic. It was battered and scratched, a field-grade model with a plastic name tag on the stock. But it felt perfect and seemed lighter and faster than his.

He tried it and hit both birds with both barrels.

"If you'd like to shoot it in the main race, you're welcome," the big man told him.

"Oh, no, but thanks," Bob said puzzled. "We're shooting against each other, aren't we?"

"No," Papa smiled, "we're shooting against the birds and the throwers."

They walked back to the main ring, and Bob noticed the shooting had stopped.

"End of the two-bird relay," Minor explained. "Now you'll see another show."

The judge stood up, waved his arm, and instantly a thundering herd of Mexican boys surged into the ring from all directions, picking up the dead birds, scrambling and fighting with each other for them. Within a matter of minutes, the ring was clean and the boys were running back into the mesquite trees behind the ring, carrying their prizes home with them.

"That's another misconception about these pigeon shoots," Minor was saying. "The birds are not wasted, and, as a matter of fact, if they're properly cooked they're fine eating. Most of the shoots in the states give them to institutions, orphanages and so forth."

When his next turn came, Bob almost forgot and loaded his gun walking out into the ring, and he was still thinking about the judge's warning when a big blue pigeon with a white dot on its tail went sizzling off low across the ring. He got tail feathers the first shot, saw the barrel jump out ahead and under the diving bird in desperation, and the bird folded cleanly. He thanked God for his own gun, it just pointed itself at times like that. Suddenly he felt a surge of confidence, and the next bird exploded inches over the rope into a shower of feathers.

The day dragged on, and on. It seemed hours between times to shoot. His fifth and sixth birds both flew slowly in the noon heat and he got them easily. Numbers seven and eight were not much more difficult, and he was lucky on number ten, a tremendously strong bird which fell and skidded almost to the outside fence one hundred meters away. Had it fallen another five yards out, beyond the row of plastic flags, it would have been a miss.

The old man in the blue sweater was standing there first in line to shake his hand. "Great shot on a tough bird," he smiled. "You really poled it to him."

"I don't know how I missed the first time."

The old man leaned forward in his ear. "You were trying to be a little careful, I think," he whispered. "If you don't mind I'll make a suggestion."

"I'd really appreciate it, sir."

"Well, forget the gun on the first shot and just really concentrate on seeing the bird clearly; the gun will get there."

Bob walked back through the crowd, and people he had never seen began asking him if he had missed, and telling him to hang on because the last day would be the hardest.

One old-timer with white hair and a beautiful Boss over-under cradled across his lap stopped him and asked the same question.

"Straight, huh?" he drawled. "Well, I always think what my daddy told me; longer a man goes without a miss at pigeons, the closer he's gettin' to one; nobody kills 'em all."

Bob thought about that, and felt tension knot his stomach again.

Minor came up behind him, furious. "You're getting the needle now," he said loudly enough for everyone around to hear. "But fortunately, most of the shooters are gentlemen and you'll just have to ignore the others."

At the end of the day there were four shooters remaining without a miss, and that night Bob turned and tossed and saw pigeons darting and dipping over the rope in his dreams.

But on the firing line the next morning, he felt more confident and his birds seemed slower and easier.

"You're picking 'em up better," Minor told him. "Hang in there, two of the other straights have already missed."

The passage of time became eternal, but his confidence grew with every bird. He kept telling himself these had to be easier than doves, and he only had two more to go.

Suddenly there was a great cheering and hand clapping in the crowd.

"Papa came through!" somebody yelled. "Twenty straight, at his age, that's something."

Bob turned to Minor with a raised eyebrow.

"I'm glad he made it, son," Minor said. "Now there's the greatest of them all, and a gentleman with it. He's got more pride than any competitor I've ever seen at anything, and that's why it's been hurting him so to hear them say he's over the hill. He had some sickness, his eyes had to be operated on, and he's getting on up in years. But he knows where to point that shotgun, and he's proved it to them one more time."

"He's still got to beat me," Bob said suddenly, and Minor glanced sidewise at him quickly.

"You've got some pride too, don't you, son? Well, you remember this, you've got the reflexes and the youth, but he's got the experience. Don't count any chickens yet."

When he went out to shoot the last two birds, Bob's knees were jelly, his throat was tight, and his fingers were shaking when he tried to load the gun. He remembered what the old man had told him, to look at the pigeon, nothing else, not the thrower, nor the gun, to concentrate on the bird.

The thrower looked him over slowly, looked down at some penciled numbers on the white leg of his pants. Bob had heard the throwers kept tabs on shooters who had not missed, working harder on them as a baseball pitcher works hardest on the big hitters. He knew he was in for a tough bird.

"*Listo?*"

"Pull." It was as if someone else had said it for him. He saw the windup, heard the thrower grunt loudly, and a black streak cleared the rope and was suddenly the size of a mosquito, sleek and swift, and disappearing.

He felt the gun go twice, saw feathers fly both times, and the bird kept flying, wings still beating wildly as it crashed full speed into the ground two feet from the hundred-meter fence.

He heard the crowd clapping. Then there was tense silence. This was it, his moment of truth. In the background he heard the mariachis and they were playing the music of the bull ring. Perhaps they were playing it for the *colombaire* who was their hero as much as a matador.

The windup was slow, deceptively graceful, a fake to the right and a full reverse, discus style. He heard the bird whistling through the air past his nose, realized he had been caught off balance, and the bird was a disappearing dot which, miraculously, almost stopped in midair, turned and started back. He waited trembling, pulled two feet ahead with the barrel, and saw the explosion of feathers and he knew he had done it. He had tied the greatest of them all!

People and faces swirled around him, hands were shaking his, Minor was hugging him around the shoulders. "We can't lose now, boy," he was yelling. "Even second place is worth a pile of money to both of us. The pressure's off."

The judge was announcing that there would be a sudden-death shoot-off for the championship, and Minor was running up with more shells.

"Take your time," he whispered. "First prize is an eight-hundred-dollar shotgun, you know."

Bob wished to hell he didn't know. He felt the tightness come back in his throat.

"Don't choke now," someone said jokingly, putting the needle back into place again.

The old man was already sitting on the ready bench, looking as cool as if he were there to watch someone else shoot for the International Championship. But when Bob sat down beside him, he saw a steely, determined look in the watery blue eyes which frightened him more than all the needling.

"Good luck," Papa said, sticking out his hand.

The judge called for the old man to shoot first, and he took his time, walking ponderously and almost wearily out to the line, methodically checking his safety, adjusting his shooting glasses, kicking a spent shell from underfoot.

The bird went whistling over the rope, took a steep cut to the left, and disintegrated into a puff of feathers.

Bob felt his pulse pounding. He could hear little things in the crowd behind him, recognized voices. "Even money he misses the first bird," somebody said.

He could hear Minor's voice. "Shut up and let the kid shoot!"

The bird was brown, and fast, driving straight away, but the barrel of the worn automatic centered itself on the V of the departing wings and he saw the bird slump and die instantly with the first shot. He pulled the trigger to put the clincher shot into him, flinched, and the gun failed to fire.

A murmur went up from the crowd.

"Hold up your gun, don't touch it," the judge yelled.

The automatic had jammed, the spent hull was sticking halfway out of the chamber. The judge checked it, cleared it, and handed it back to him.

"Would you like to change guns, or fire this one into the air a couple of times to see if it will work?"

Bob took the gun, pointed it high, and both explosions jarred him.

"I'll stay with this one," he said.

The old man was deliberate, waiting for his next bird to make its downwind hooking curve, and he nicked it high the first shot, then missed clean as the bird went struggling down almost to the fence.

Bob tried to take his time, to make sure in case the gun failed again, and as he pulled the trigger the pigeon darted to the left and he knew he'd missed. He pulled the trigger again, and nothing happened. Instantly he jerked out the jammed shell, felt the action slam shut, and threw the barrel far ahead, then farther in front of the tiny dot of a bird now high in the sky and nearly out of the ring. The bird made three wingbeats, then suddenly hesitated, slumped and cartwheeled to the ground.

"Fantastic shot!" somebody yelled, and then he could barely hear the judge for the roaring of the crowd.

Papa walked out slowly again, but shot faster than before and the bird was fringed by the pattern of the first shot, ducked under the second, was heading for the fence. Bob's pulse was pounding. At the same time he wanted the bird to fall for Papa and to keep going for him and the eight-hundred-dollar gun. The bird kept flying, gradually losing altitude, and crashed into the wire fence of the ring.

"Let's have a runner check the bird," the judge yelled.

A Mexican boy ran out into the ring straight for the pigeon, which was up and walking. If he could retrieve the bird, it would be a kill. If the bird could fly out, the International Championship could belong to Bob Bernard.

The bird hopped into the air, fluttered almost to the fence, and the boy caught him in midair. A great cheer, and roar of applause came from the crowd.

Papa was walking over to him, and for the first time he noticed the old man's hands were shaking.

"If you'd like to shoot my gun," he said, "you're welcome to it. I don't believe I'd trust that one again."

Bob took the gun, still warm from its two quick shots, and with it seemed to come some of the confidence of the old man. Yet his mind whirled; what if he beat the old man with his own gun?

When he called for the bird it was as if the barrel was weighted with lead; somehow he could not make it get ahead of the bird; then it leaped out front and in that instant the bird swerved and dived wildly for the ground. He raked the bird high, saw the gyrating target go wild, pulled over it as it rose to catch the wind, and saw feathers fly. The bird was dead and the crowd was roaring. But in disbelief he watched it glide, wings set in death, as the wind blew it near and nearer the fence. "Down bird!" Minor was yelling. "Down!"

There was a split second of dead, pindrop silence. And then the white flag of a lost bird rose above the ring from all three flag-boys, and the crowd went wild.

Bob was still staring, unable to believe it nor to move nor do anything, when the old man walked up and put his arm around his shoulder.

"The new gun is yours anyway," he whispered as the crowd surged around them. "We both know you earned it . . . you've just learned that in this game, there's also a lot of luck."

But what Bob Bernard knew, in that moment, was what it takes to be a great champion at the most humbling shooting contest in the world.

"Thanks, Mr. Ilseng," he said softly, "for everything."

The Night of Manhood

Copano Bay was getting close; Roy Stanford knew it without opening his eyes. He could sense it, even in the closed car, the musky smell of salt water, the heavy humidity to the air. He wondered how old he would have to be before that sensation of nearing the coast lost its magic.

He had dozed, but not slept, all the way from San Antonio. It is not easy for a man to sleep with a sixteen-year-old son at the wheel. But Andy's driving wasn't bothering him so much now as the conversation of the eighteen-year-old on the front seat beside him.

Stephen Lee had been just another kid down the street, except maybe for the long hair, hippie glasses, and ridiculous high-heeled suede boots. Now he was beginning to wonder if this dark-haired punk with the brooding blue eyes wasn't about as dangerous to his son as a rattlesnake.

He felt the tires crunch gravel as Andy swerved off the highway onto the road to the bay. He'd been driving too fast all the way, and that swerving off the highway was to impress Stephen.

"Pretty quick trip, huh?" Andy said.

"The trip I'd like to be on right now," said Stephen, "would be with a little acid and some neat chick."

Feigning sleep, Roy thought he understood the words. But he couldn't be sure with the radio blaring soul music as loud as it would go.

"Andy, turn down that damn radio a little!"

The boy turned around and grinned at his father, stretching like a lithe, tawny cat . . . six feet of boyhood stretched over the frame of a man.

"Aw, you just wake up and the first thing you do is gripe. You're sure gettin' old and crabby."

"Well, since I'm so old and crabby, how come we're already to Copano; I suppose you kept your toe in the carburetor all the way?"

"It was really a pretty slow scene, man," Stephen mumbled, slouching farther down into the seat, hat over his eyes. "We got passed by four buses, a milk truck and a donkey cart."

Roy felt his temperature rising, and took a deep breath. It wasn't so much being called "man" instead of "sir," it was the tone, the utter contempt in it.

Stephen was just getting started.

"Tell me something," he asked. "What if you caught every flounder in this world, I mean like tubs and piles of flounder? Would that make you guys happy, or do you do it for the sport, or what? I mean, it's like they only make one model of flounder, right? And you just go on year after year stickin' the same old flounder on that same little spear. I don't get the kick, man."

"So why did you ask to come along, Stephen?" Roy asked.

"Grounded, man," he groaned. "No grades, no wheels. It's like staying home with mamma, and if it's mamma or mosquitos, I gotta go with the bugs you can spray."

Andy looked at his father anxiously; he'd seen that red-headed temper flare over a lot less.

But Roy's voice was even. "I really can't explain why men enjoy floundering or fishing, Stephen. It's possibly some pre-historic instinct some of us have and others don't. But I've found that in life, the best things often are those you don't fully under-stand and just don't question."

Andy turned off the gravel road onto the grassy shoreline where they'd camped since he was a toddler, and began unloading the equipment.

Roy got out, stretched, and walked over to Stephen. "I'm going to tell you exactly as I told your father. You asked to go, and Andy enjoys your company. Fine. But I've got the responsi-bility of you while you're with me, and you're going to have to do what I say, without question and without argument. A lot of things can happen out in that bay at night, and there may not be time for me to argue with you. I'm not going to argue with you, in fact. Do you understand, Stephen?"

"What things could happen out there?"

Andy tried to intercede because he saw his father's face reddening.

"Stingrays," Andy said. "They got enough poison in their tails to rot off your leg if they hit you. And sawfish, they look like great big sharks, except they have this big, flat spear with sharp saw teeth on it, and when they swim that spear is cuttin' back and forth like a machete. They come up in the shallow water at night, and if you happen to spook one, he's liable to get excited and run right over you. I guess they could cut your legs right out from under you if they did. We saw one last year that looked fourteen feet long!"

Stephen was looking off at the horizon someplace.

"I don't see you guys hobbling around on one leg."

Roy had enough. "You can go, or you can sit in the car," he said. "But if you go, I'm the boss, starting right now."

Andy knew that tone of voice. He nudged Stephen toward the water.

They spread out, thirty yards apart, slowly walking the hard slope of sand dropping off into a deeper gut of the bay. Roy showed Stephen how to slide his feet, to minimize the chance of stepping down on a stingray, and sent Andy on across the gut to work the far shoreline.

For half an hour they walked slowly, Stephen temporarily fascinated by the strange sights and creatures turning up in the flickering circle of light of the lamp. White cabbagehead jellyfish undulated in the current; crabs threw up their claws in their ludicrous Archie Moore defense, then ran sidewise or backwards out of the way. Once a big fish rushed up to the light, eyes shining in the glare, and was gone.

When he saw the first flounder, Stephen almost didn't see it, just a brown lump of bottom, half covered with sand. Then it squirted away in a cloud of silt. The next one he saw, he took careful aim and jammed the spear through it, feeling the gig vibrating and seeing the mud obscure it instantly.

Purposely without waiting, he reached down, felt its gills as Andy told him, and picked it up, holding it against the spear.

Roy had been watching, and he almost wished it had been a ray.

They worked the shore down to the mouth of a small slough with boggy, sulphurous mud at its mouth which was deep and murky from schools of mullet swarming its ledge. Roy went one way, sending Stephen the other, and it was Roy who jumped the monster.

He leaped back suddenly, light swinging in the air, and yelled for Stephen to get out of the way. Instead, Stephen raised his spear.

"Stephen, listen to me," Roy was yelling. "Do not, do not try to stick that thing."

Stephen wished whatever it was would come by, just so he could stick it. And suddenly he saw the water bulging at the edge of the ring of light, then a flat, saw-toothed bill and the huge, ugly body of a giant sawfish. It passed him at the edge of the deeper water, and he took careful aim and threw the spear with all his might into the body just behind the head.

All hell broke loose; mud and water flew. Ten feet and two hundred pounds of frightened, maddened sawfish turned and did exactly as Roy knew he would. He headed for deep water, and he was heading straight for Roy, trapped in the small pass between the flat and the channel. Roy tried to run backward, the bulge in the water was upon him in an instant, and he tried to leap back out of the way, feeling in the same instant the brute force hitting him, hearing the crash of the giant tail exploding the

surface, feeling water swirling into ears and eyes and mud in his face as he rolled away from it, gasping for air, and getting his feet under him again and feeling them go out again.

Stephen was running over to him and Roy stood up unsteadily. Suddenly all the suppressed fears and hates of pot, protest, Castro beards and Beatle haircuts, dirty kids and amplified noise boiled up inside him, and somehow he had Stephen by the arms in a grip of granite, shaking him as a lion shakes a mouse, slapping him full in the face.

"That," he bellowed, "is for your mother who suffered you into this world, and that's for the sweat of whoever farmed the food and built the shelter to keep a parasite like you alive on this earth, and that's for your father who never had the guts to give it to you himself!"

Stephen was taking it, not fighting, not ducking, just taking it. Blood ran down his nose, and there was a strange look of disbelief on his face.

Roy held him close, eye to eye, and squeezed his arms in the crushing grip of a man who works with his hands. "Now so help me God, you miserable punk, you stay away from Andy or I'll break every rotten bone in your bored little body!"

Stephen had never dropped his lantern. He was looking down at the water, the dark blackness of blood coming from beneath Roy, watching him with a strange look of awe.

"We gotta get you out of here, fast," he said.

"Sawfish cut me, I expect," said Roy, suddenly remarkably calm, the hate gone from him, leaving him weak, and for the first time he felt the sting of the salt water in his leg and the giddiness and sickness of shock.

The boy raised his lantern and saw the leg was laid bare to the bone, the flap of muscle and flesh undulating uselessly in the current, blood pouring from the wound. Stephen stripped off his shirt, quickly cut one long sleeve from it, and made a tourniquet. He had read how to do a fireman's carry someplace, and his mind raced. Roy weighed two hundred pounds.

"I think I can carry you out, Mr. Stanford," he said, "if you'll hold the lantern and just lean forward over my shoulder."

As he straightened up under the weight, Stephen felt his feet break through the crust of bottom into the mire. He stumbled and lunged forward, caught his balance again, and headed straight for the shoreline.

"You can't cut across here, son," Roy grunted. "This shoreline's alive with stingrays. They're spawning now."

"I'll have to take my chances," said Stephen. "It's the shortest way."

He felt the hard bottom change to soft silt. Twice he saw clouds of mud in the wavering light of the lantern ahead, but his eyes were on the shoreline and he leaned forward and made better time, wondering if he had enough breath, enough guts to make it.

Andy saw the single light bobbing erratically and moving straight across the stingray flat. He began running in the shallow water.

Stephen's legs were turning to rubber, his lungs were bursting and he felt the overpowering urge to just fall forward into the water and give up. Red dots chased across his eyes, and he was staggering in the mud. But the salt grass of the shoreline was nearer and nearer.

Andy was there, gasping for breath, running out in the water to meet them, sharing the load, half shoving, half carrying his father to shore. Roy had begun blacking out.

The station wagon careened on two wheels up the shell road toward Rockport, with Roy stretched across the back seat. Andy drove while Stephen tightened and loosened the sodden tourniquet.

In the emergency room of the little hospital, Roy got plasma and morphine, and it was only when the young intern, working fast but efficiently, told the boys he was out of danger that Stephen suddenly slumped forward to the floor.

Andy grabbed him and a nurse propped him in a chair.

"I think," said Stephen, the sweat of pain and nausea popping out on his lips and forehead, "one of those damn stingrays got me in the leg."

"Which one?" the nurse asked quickly.

"I dunno," Stephen smiled weakly. "See one of those kooky things and you've seen 'em all."

The intern began cutting Stephen's right pants leg; he could see the ugly swelling at a glance.

They were both feeling much better the next morning when the two families drove in from San Antonio, Stephen's father anxious to move his boy immediately to better facilities.

"If you don't mind, sir, I'd just as soon stay here with Mr. Stanford; between the two of us, we've got one good pair of legs to get to the bathroom."

"What's all this 'sir' and 'mister' stuff, coming from you?" his mother said curiously, feeling his forehead for fever. "Did you decide to rejoin the establishment or something?"

"No," smiled Stephen, "not exactly. It's like last night Mr. Stanford just sort of explained it all to me, ma'am."

One Very Fine Doe

The sky sagged in heavy, gray billows, ready to give way at the seams, and the freshening wind was heavy with the smell of rain already falling somewhere across the cactus and oak mott hills.

Luke Roberts manhandled the steering wheel and dropped the high-wheeled old pickup into four-wheel drive to climb the rocky grade, wondering how long it would be before the per- fumed little lady sitting between them in the lurching cab was going to announce to her boy friend that she'd had enough of this deer hunting.

"Ma'am," he was saying as if somebody had asked, "this country is changing so fast the coyotes don't know whether to howl nor holler. This ranch used to be a working cattle ranch, with a few sheep and goats here on the upper end where it's too rough for cattle range. But now it's a regular zoo; the boss is like a lot of these old Texas country boys, poor at English but fair at arithmetic. He can make more money raising this exotic game, shipping it in here from all over the world, letting it go wild and then selling hunting rights. And it's a lot easier'n workin' cattle."

The mustached man from New York was not in the least interested in the status of the ranch's game other than the trophy buck deer he had come to shoot on a no-kill, no-pay basis.

"When are we going to stop driving and start hunting?" He glanced impatiently at the diamond-encrusted watch on his wrist, stirring up a strong aroma of men's cologne. "We've got to catch a plane in San Antonio this afternoon."

Luke dodged a rock and pointed out to the lady a couple of doe standing, ears up and necks craning in curiosity on the next ridge.

"We're huntin' right now," he said casually. "I'm working my way up to that ridge over there and we'll get out and rattle the horns. That's the territory of a real good buck I've been seeing up here all season. 'Course, you know deer are like kids and girl friends, they hardly ever show off just right in front of strangers."

The girl, who had short blond hair, a voluptuous down jacket, and tight Western jeans from Fifth Avenue, didn't understand a bit about rattling up the buck. But she was beginning to enjoy the dry easy mastery this wedge-shouldered Texan was developing over a sage of the stock market.

"An old buck is about like an old man," Luke advised. "He sort of stakes out his territory, and he's mighty jealous of any other buck that gets into it. I'll show you directly how he marks off his country with horn scrapes and where he paws the ground and such, to inform any doe passing through the country that he's available. He's also warning off any other bucks that might take a liking to the territory or one of his girl friends, and that's why this horn rattlin' works so well. We just make the sounds of two bucks knockin' heads and fightin' over a doe, and if there's a big buck around he's got to come and investigate."

"I'm surprised you can't talk one up," the man said acidly.

"Well," Luke said, "where I was raised the nearest doctor was forty miles off an' mamma had to protect all the kids from smallpox herself. Wasn't my fault she vaccinated me with a phonograph needle."

The girl giggled, the mustached man scowled and looked out the window.

Just short of the rim of the ridge, Luke stopped the truck, picked up the battered binoculars and scanned the countryside. "Just want to make sure the old buck isn't lookin' right at us from the next hill over there. He's likely bedded down in that thick canyon on the other side, and with the wind this way, he's liable to run right over us. Reckon you can defend us?"

The man from New York groaned audibly.

"How can you know where a deer is going to run? Didn't you say this ranch covers about a hundred square miles?"

"Well, I guess New York has a few people in it, too," Luke drawled good-naturedly, "but I'll gamble that you know pretty well where this little gal is gonna be most of the time."

The man couldn't decide if "deer rattling" was one of Luke Roberts' put-ons or not, but he took the scoped .375 magnum carefully out of its fitted case.

Luke looked at the gun, noticed that it would shine like a warning mirror in the sun, and shook his head at the size of the hole in the barrel. "In case we jump a polar bear," he decided, "we'll be set for him."

They walked up the hill, Luke's scuffed cowboy boots taking it easy, the others rolling rocks. The man from New York was walking head up and chin out, getting ahead, as if he were beating the crowd to a subway station.

"If you'd slow up just a mite," Luke drawled, "the little lady and I could keep up, and I also might be able to see whether the wind is right for this spot right here."

He picked a big tree with thick brush around the base of it, and enough hillside behind to break up their outline. He put the man over to the right, with the tree between them just in case the cannon went off, and the girl behind in a clump of brush where her fluttering white scarf wouldn't be quite so obvious.

Then he began breaking off limbs and brush, making a little opening where he could kneel and rattle the horns, and the New Yorker grumbled about the noise.

"Well, we're settin' up a phony deer fight here, mister, and the first thing a couple of bucks do is square off and break up a little brush, hookin' at it and showin' how tough they are. And you don't have to whisper yet, that old buck is a half-mile over yonder in that thicket, if he's here at all. Main thing is just to be still; don't move a hair until you come up to shoot."

"Why don't the deer see us?" the girl asked, getting interested and believing the story.

"Well, a deer's color-blind, you know," Luke explained, "and I got enough cover behind us to break up our outlines. And then, the way he'll be comin' he won't get a really straight look at us. An old buck usually circles to get the wind on anything he's not sure of; he trusts his nose more'n his eyes. But he don't like crossing openings in daytime, which is why I set us up here with that opening straight downwind. In order to circle and get the scent of the fight he hears going on, he'll likely try and hold to heavy cover long as he can, and as he circles through those trees right yonder, he'll have to all but run right over us."

"Could we do something rather than just talking about it?" the New Yorker demanded. "Doesn't time mean anything at all to you people down here?"

"Sure," Luke grinned. "We think enough of it to make sure we always have plenty."

He clashed the horns together hard, twisting and pulling them apart, to create the rattling, gnashing noise of two bucks coming together head on. He kicked a rock and sent it rolling down the hillside, hit one horn against the rough bark of the tree and ripped it down, making all the noise available in that particular thicket. Then he rested the horns on the ground, dropped to one knee, and waited.

He clashed the horns twice more before there was a gray movement on the next hillside, then the bobbing rack of antlers, and a magnificent buck stepped out into the edge of the clearing.

"He's too far," Luke said softly. "Give him time."

The buck stood head up, scanning the hillside, then lowered his head and began sneaking through the trees.

"He's gone," the New Yorker said, starting to get up.

"Git down!" Luke hissed in a tone the New Yorker could understand. A second later the buck broke out almost on top of them in a lope, head up, hair on his neck swelled in anger, looking for a fight.

The New Yorker's mouth gaped, the buck stood glaring at them at twenty paces.

"Shoot!"

The buck stood, shaking his antlers, unable to comprehend the creatures he could now see but not quite make out.

"Shoot, dammit!"

Suddenly the buck whirled, gave one magnificent leap over a cactus clump, and disappeared into the thicket.

Luke stood up, reached for a cigarette, and offered one to the girl.

The New Yorker's face was brilliant red behind the mustache.

"He wasn't big enough," he said. "I thought you had some real trophy bucks on this ranch."

"Well," drawled Luke, "I counted about fifteen points on that one, and I figure he'd go twenty-two inches or so across the horns. If he'd been any bigger you'd need an elk license."

They got back into the pickup, and the New Yorker announced he would hunt on foot, in the manner to which he was accustomed, and that Luke could take the girl and maybe rattle up a buck for her if she wanted to shoot one.

"Yessir," said Luke. "I'll pick you up after a while at that

windmill over yonder on the next hill; it's the highest place around here and you can't get lost as long as you keep in sight of it."

They bounced off across the hills, back to the main road and into another pasture, where he could show the girl some wild turkeys and some blackbuck antelope from India.

The rain, which had been rumbling and threatening all morning, suddenly let loose with a downpour, and they stopped the truck and watched a doe with twin fawns bounce stiff-legged and daintily across into the protection of a cedar-rimmed canyon.

The girl told him how much she wanted to have children someday, preferably twins, but that she'd just about decide this guy never was even going to the altar.

Luke showed her a Mexican eagle sitting in a tree, a jackrabbit, and a covey of quail under a cactus. And then the rain really poured, a blinding, insulating curtain capsuling the world to the cab of the truck, where it was warm, and where she learned that ranch hands have calluses, but gentle ways, and it was well after the rain stopped that they remembered the man from New York didn't even have a raincoat.

When they got to the windmill, the sun was out bright and warm and he was waiting on a big rock, drenched but triumphant, making a show of sharpening his big-bladed knife on a rock.

"Got me one of those big rams you were talking about," he said, trying to seem nonchalant about it, "and also a big mule deer doe. Frankly, I thought she had horns; she was standing under a bush and it looked like the trophy I came down here after. But doe are legal here, aren't they?"

"Sure are," Luke said. "Better eatin' than a buck anyway. By the way, you know the ranch charges two-fifty for one of those rams, but that's cheaper than going to Corsica to get one, and that doe won't cost you but fifty."

"The money isn't important," the man snapped. "I just wish I could have gotten a real trophy buck. But that doe I got was twice the size of that little so-called trophy you rattled up this morning. I thought I'd never get her field-dressed."

"Oh?" said Luke. "Well, I'll drive you all back to the ranch house and I'll send a Mexican up here to get the ram and the doe; you marked where they are like I told you, didn't you?"

"Oh yes," the New Yorker said, "they're both right by the windmill; I saw a lot of game right in there. Anyone should know that the game in this godforsaken country would be close to water."

Luke let them out, gave the girl a quick little pat on the rear when the man wasn't looking, caught her wink, and drove down to the bunkhouse to get Manuel.

"Go up there to the Paint Creek windmill," he told the Mexican, "and pick up a ram my hunter killed this morning. Then go by the freezer and pick out about a hundred pounds of deer meat, all different cuts, and if there isn't enough, throw in a few chunks of goat. We gotta send him back with a pile of eatin' meat of some kind.

"And, Manuel, when you come by that old mare mule up by the windmill, tie onto her with the pickup and drag her up over the hill someplace out of sight, and keep your mouth shut about it. And if that man from New York says anything to you, brag on him a little and tell him that was the biggest doe you ever had to skin out in your whole life, you *comprende*, Manuel?"